NEW ORLEANS

NOCTURNES

# CARRIE PULKINEN

Shift Happens

Contact Information: www.CarriePulkinen.com

Cover Art by Rebecca Poole of Dreams2Media
Edited by Krista Venero of Mountains Wanted

First Edition, 2020
ISBN: 978-0-9998436-9-7

**She wants to bang a werewolf, not become one.**

Sophie Burroughs is determined to be a witch. Her grandmother was a witch. All the other supes say she smells like a witch, but she can't cast a spell to save her life.

Sprouting fur is *so* not on her to-do list.

But when a smokin' hot werewolf bites her and then accuses her of crimes against his pack, she has until the next full moon to prove him wrong and stop his magic from transforming her into a wolf.

A romp in the sack would be a nice bonus, too.

Trace Thibodeaux didn't mean to bite Sophie. The red wolves have been cursed, she's the prime suspect, and if he wants to keep his rank in the pack, he has to end her magic by any means necessary.

But that doesn't include sheathing his sword in a witch's scabbard.

He's gotten into bed with the enemy before, and that's a mistake he'll never make again.

Or will he?

CHAPTER ONE

"If doing this buck naked doesn't work, I don't know what will." Sophie Burroughs dropped her blue silk robe onto the back of a chair and smoothed a soiled shirt on the kitchen table. She ran her finger over her grandmother's handwritten incantation in the grimoire, tapping the line beneath the title. "It says, 'A simple spell to remove stains from clothing.' Simplicity must be the key, and you can't get any simpler than being buck naked."

"I think the preferred term is 'skyclad.'" Jane, her vampire best friend, leaned against the wall, peering at Sophie's ancestral book. "And I don't think being naked is going to make it any easier to cast a spell."

"Hey, being naked makes a lot of things easier. Sex. Shaving. You don't have to do laundry." She ticked the list off on her fingers. "Anyway, I read about this online. Some witches perform their spells naked because it intensifies their magic. Maybe my grandma was one of them."

Jane scrunched her nose. "Ew. Now I'm picturing a wrinkly old lady with sagging boobs dancing naked around a bonfire. Thanks."

"She was twenty-five when she died, and she was gorgeous. I've seen pictures."

"I still don't think it's going to help."

"You never know until you try." Sophie scanned the short incantation one more time, though she'd already memorized it during the first seven times she tried to cast the damn spell.

Jane grabbed her boobs through her red cashmere sweater, pushing them together and up before narrowing her eyes at Sophie's. "I should have gotten implants while I was alive. Yours are fabulous."

"Oh, please." She waved a hand dismissively. "Yours will stay perky for all eternity, while I've got about twenty years tops before gravity comes a-callin'. Besides, the hottest vampire in New Orleans thinks you're utterly perfect, so I don't want to hear it." Sophie jerked her head toward the exit. "Either get naked or get out. I don't want anything contaminating this spell. It has to work this time."

Jane lifted her hands, a look of pity softening her eyes. "I'll be in the living room." She flipped her long, dark hair over her shoulder and strutted out of the kitchen.

Sophie closed her eyes, taking a deep breath and trying her damnedest to sense some kind of magic sparking inside her. Nothing happened, as usual, but she ignored the empty sensation like she ignored her best friend's looks of sympathy every time one of her grandma's spells refused to be cast. Which was literally *every* time.

If she could just get one to work—any spell, it didn't matter which at this point—she could prove she belonged in the coven and finally get those secretive bitches—err... witches—to accept her. It was her destiny. A palm reader told her so.

Focusing on the stain, she recited the spell three times, each repetition growing louder, intensifying along with her frustration. As she ended the final chant, she swiped her hand across the fabric, exactly like the directions told her to do, and waited, willing the damn spot to disappear. Nothing happened.

"Fuck me with a wooden dildo. I give up." She jabbed her arms into the robe sleeves, cinching the belt around her waist before dropping into a chair.

"The Sophie I know never gives up." Jane appeared in the doorway faster than Sophie could blink and sank into the chair next to her. Damn vampires and their super-speed. They could also wipe a person's mind and make them dumber than a turkey lining up for Thanksgiving dinner—at least for a short period of time. It was so unfair.

"Meet the new Sophie, quitter extraordinaire." She crossed her arms, and as her bottom lip poked out in a pout, she left it there. Even badass bitches deserved a little pity party every now and then.

Jane shook her head, leaning an elbow on the table and flashing that look of pity again. "You're not a quitter. You moved five hundred miles away from home to expand your business on the advice of a fortune teller, and you're doing great. This magic stuff is weird. A lot of it boils down to fate and meant-to-be crap that I never believed in before, but listen…" She grasped Sophie's hand. "You can't force it. If you're meant to have powers, they'll come when it's time. Good goat cheese, do you hear me? I'm starting to sound like Ethan."

"Great. And in the meantime, I'll just stay the awkward weirdo who gets along better with animals than she does people." She touched the scabbed-over bite marks on her forearm. "Most animals."

Jane rolled her eyes. "I'm married to a drama queen. I don't need this shit from my best friend too. You and I both know you're not a weirdo; lots of people are good with animals, and that's a werewolf bite. It doesn't count."

She pulled her sleeve down, covering the wound. "Whoever it was, they were in animal form when they bit me. Has Gaston had any luck figuring out who did it?"

"None. Apparently, it's illegal for werewolves to bite witches without permission, and since you smell like a witch and had a witch grandmother, the entire supernatural community is being tight-lipped about it."

She leaned an elbow on the table, resting her chin in her hand. "Fabulous." The one time they acted like Sophie was actually a witch, she didn't want them to.

"How's it healing? Do you need me to lick it again?"

"It's fine." Sophie laughed. Vampire spit had healing properties, but she would never get used to hearing Jane talk about this stuff like it was the most normal thing in the world. "My best friend just offered to lick my wounds. Maybe I'm not the weirdo in this pair after all."

"You're definitely not."

Sophie sighed and flipped the grimoire shut. The leather spine creaked as the cover closed over the thousand-plus pages of secrets Sophie apparently wasn't meant to be privy to. "I think I've found a witch who might be willing to help me. She lives upstairs and runs the coffee shop on the first floor."

"Are you sure she's a witch? Have you asked her?"

"Not yet. She's kinda my last hope, so I'm giving it time, getting to know her before I start bombarding her with questions."

Jane nodded, tapping a finger to her temple. "Smart."

"I just can't believe I did this, you know?"

"Did what?"

She toyed with the belt on her robe. "Moved here on the advice of a psychic."

Jane patted her hand. "You also moved here to be with your BFF."

"I know, but I got so caught up in the apparent magic of the situation, I couldn't see it for what it really was. A coincidence."

"You've always been a believer, and that psychic did come highly recommended. I read the reviews after you saw her."

Sophie had seen a palm reader on a whim one night when she was out with a few of her employees. After a flourish of ringing bells and chanting in a language Sophie didn't understand, the psychic told her that her business would prosper in New Orleans and if she went there, she'd find magic and a man who'd make her innermost dreams come true.

The very next day, Jane had told her she was planning a trip to the French Quarter for Mardi Gras, and Sophie pounced at the chance to make the palm reader's premonition come true.

Now, her dog walking business was doing well, and she'd found magic alright. Her best friend was turned into a vampire the second night they were there, but the witches in the tourist shops wouldn't give Sophie a hot minute, much less the time of day.

New Orleans was full of supernatural beings, but they blended in with the humans, leaving Sophie dancing around the edges of a magical world she wanted so badly to join. And the man who would make her innermost dreams come true? Yeah, right. Aside from the hunk she'd encountered briefly—and quickly lost—at the party last night, she hadn't met a single man remotely capable of making her orgasm, much less making her dreams come true.

That palm reader must have had her wires crossed, because the prophecy didn't come true for Sophie, it happened for her best friend.

"Ugh." Sophie angled her head toward the sky. "God, Grandma Burroughs. Why did you have to die before you could teach me how to be a witch?" Her jaw clenched shut, and she shoved the grimoire away from her. The book slid across the smooth wood tabletop, teetering on the edge before falling to the floor with a thunk. Damn, that little hissy fit felt good.

"Careful. That's an old book." Jane slipped out of her chair and crouched on the floor to retrieve it. "Hey, Soph? Have you read the whole thing?"

"It's more than a thousand pages. I haven't made it past the basic stuff." And it seemed she never would. It was time to face the facts. Sophie just wasn't a witch.

Jane rose onto her knees, peering at her friend over the kitchen table. "A year ago, I wouldn't have thought anything of this, but I think you need to come see the page it fell open to."

"Why? Is it a spell to create the perfect man, because I think I found that in my cookbook. Gingerbread men. They're quiet, sweet, and if they get on your nerves, you can bite their heads off." She plopped cross-legged on the floor next to Jane.

"Look at the date on this." Jane pointed to the script in the top right corner. "Wasn't your dad born in 1963?"

Sophie nodded. "She wrote this spell a week after his birthday."

Four lines of elegant cursive writing were positioned in the center of the otherwise blank, yellowing page.

> *My heir will land where the Spanish reigned.*
> *When man turns beast, her path will be forged.*
> *What is done will be undone.*
> *All must be lost to find everything.*

"What the hell is that supposed to mean? I thought spells had to rhyme." Sophie scanned the text again. "'My heir will land where the Spanish reigned?' That doesn't sound like an incantation."

Jane picked up the grimoire, gently placing it on the table. "I think it's a prophecy." She turned the page. Finding it blank, she turned the next one, and then another. "The book is empty after this."

"Because she died shortly after my dad was born." Sophie flipped the page back to the supposed prophecy. "Do you think it's about my dad? He's her heir, right? Her son?"

"Could be." Jane leaned over the grimoire, running her tongue over her teeth.

"Oh, hon, your fangs are out." Sophie wiggled a finger at Jane's fully extended canines. "Do you need to go?"

Jane didn't take her eyes off the book. "I'm supposed to meet Ethan at eleven for a meal, but this is too fascinating to interrupt. Do you still have my stash in your fridge?"

"There's a bottle of O positive on the bottom shelf. Last one."

Jane's lip curled as she sent a text to her husband. "I prefer O neg these days, but it'll do. I asked Ethan to pick some up on his way home."

"He doesn't mind you standing him up?" Sophie opened the fridge and took out the bottle of blood—another thing she would never get used to. The mere sight of blood made Jane faint not too long ago. She popped it in the microwave to heat it as close to 98.6 degrees as she could get it and poured herself a glass of chardonnay.

"He's with Gaston. As long as I'm home for playtime before dawn, he won't mind."

"You're so lucky." Sophie set the warmed bottle and a wine glass in front of Jane before sinking into the chair. "I'm on my third set of batteries this month."

"You know all you'd have to do is bat your lashes, and you could have any man you wanted in your bed."

This was true. Sophie had never had any trouble landing a man. It was holding on to one she hadn't mastered yet. That, and finding one who actually knew his way around a woman's body was next to impossible. If not for her trusty vibrator, she'd be wound tighter than her Spanx after an all-you-can-eat buffet. "I'm tired of casual sex. I want more. I want what you have with Ethan."

"You'll find it when the time is right. I know you will."

She could have argued, but what was the point? She'd either find Mr. Right, or she wouldn't. No use crying over milk that couldn't be spilled because it didn't even exist. "So, 'land where the Spanish reigned.' Do you think she meant Mexico? We went to Cancun once for summer vacation when I was a teenager."

Jane chewed the inside of her cheek, her brow

furrowing as she stared at the book. "I don't think this is about your dad. Read the second line."

"'When man turns beast, her path will be forged.'" Sophie gasped. "'*Her* path.' But, my dad is an only child. My grandma didn't have any female heirs."

"She has you."

"Me?" Her mouth dropped open. "How can it be about me? I wasn't even a glimmer in my dad's eye when she wrote it. He was just a baby himself."

"It's a prophecy, duh. It's about the future. Look." Jane pointed to the third line. "'When man turns beast, her path will be forged.' Soph, a werewolf bit you last night. That's the very definition of a man turned beast."

This was crazy. Sophie's dead grandmother did not write a prophecy about her thirty years before she was born. "Okay, maybe that fits, but what about the first line? 'The land where the Spanish reigned.' We're in the *French* quarter. All the cute little sayings here are in French: *lagniappe*, *laissez les bons temps*, and all that jazz. Ethan calls you *cher*, not *mi amour*."

"You haven't been on any of the walking tours since you moved here, have you?"

"I walk fifteen dogs a day. I'm not about to pay money to walk more."

Jane laughed. "The Spanish were in control of New Orleans at the end of the seventeen hundreds. Most of the architecture in the French Quarter is actually Spanish."

"Oh." Her eyes widened, and she straightened her spine. "Oh my God. We flew here the first time, so I did technically *land* where the Spanish reigned." A flurry of adrenaline rolled through her veins, making her heart pound. "A man did turn into a beast, and then the sucker bit me. But what's my path?" She clutched Jane's shoulders, her voice coming out in a whisper. "What's my path, Jane?"

"I don't know. Maybe you're really going to turn into a werewolf?"

Gaston, their three-hundred-year-old vampire friend, informed Sophie there was a 99% chance the bite would heal, and Sophie could get on with her life. But since her ancestor was a witch, she might have had a little dormant magic inside her that could activate the werewolf mutation and make her sprout fur at the next full moon.

Wouldn't that be her luck? She wanted to sleep with a werewolf, not become one herself. "I obviously don't have any magic, or I'd be able to get one of these spells to work."

"Read the next line." Jane pointed to the book. "'What's done will be undone.' What do you think that means?"

"It'll be undone. The bite will heal, and I won't turn into a werewolf." That had to be what it meant. Sophie was intent on becoming a witch, not a werewolf. She loved animals more than she loved people, but hair only belonged on her head and between her legs. She refused to sprout fur. It wasn't ladylike.

Jane poured the blood into the glass and swirled it like a fine wine. "That sounds feasible. It makes sense if you think about it."

"It does. Definitely."

"So, all that's left is the last line. 'All must be lost to find everything.'" Jane took a swig of O positive and grimaced. "That doesn't sound promising."

"Okay, but everything else has been vague. I mean, 'when man becomes beast.' If we'd read this a year ago, that wouldn't have made a lick of sense either. None of it would have. Maybe I'm going to lose my purse, and when someone returns it, I'll buy a lottery ticket because I'll be feeling so lucky. Then I'll win."

Jane arched a brow. "That's a stretch."

"It could happen."

"I guess."

"Anyway, the important thing right now is that I'm *not* going to turn into a werewolf. It says so right here." She jabbed her finger at the third line of the prophecy. "And the path that has been forged is my way to becoming a witch. I was ready to give up, but now I have a renewed drive. 'All must be lost' is so vague, it could have already happened. Hell, maybe it happened tonight. I'd lost my will to continue, and now I've found a reason to go on. That's it!"

Sophie closed the book and stood, parking her hands on her hips. "I figured it out. I'm going to become a witch, and the only werewolf I'll ever have in me is the massive dick of the one who's going to make my innermost dreams come true."

Jane laughed. "You go, girl. Grab your destiny by the cock…I mean horns."

"Who's Destiny?" Sophie grinned. "Oh, that's right. She's my bitch."

CHAPTER TWO

S he smelled like a witch. Five male dogs, at least three of them alphas, strolled along in a semicircle around her without so much as a raised hackle or growl of warning, and that feat in itself would require mad magical powers. That many males never got along so peacefully, especially tethered together like they were.

She had to be a witch—an unregistered one, the most dangerous kind. And he was the dumbass who bit her.

Trace Thibodeaux crouched behind a trash can on St. Philip Street, looking like a lunatic as he observed the woman walking the dogs. Sophie Burroughs. Her warm cinnamon and cider witch scent drifted on the breeze, igniting a fire inside him the way it did the night he met her. But now, a slight woodsy hint tainted the fragrance, an indication that his magic was mixing with hers, possibly turning her into a werewolf by the next full moon.

If she was the one responsible for the hell that had broken loose within his pack—and he was 99.9% positive she was—he could've used any means necessary to force her to lift the spell and turn over his missing friend.

*Could have.* Until, in a flash of confusion he still didn't understand, he'd bitten her, transferring his magic and possibly turning her into one of the most powerful weres alive. Sure, she'd lose the ability to cast spells if she made the shift from woman to beast, but her inborn power would remain. Anyone who had that kind of control over alphas was a threat to his kind. He'd screwed up royally, and now he had to do something about it.

That was what he got for mixing business with pleasure.

She turned the corner with her pack of leashed dogs, and Trace straightened, shoving his hands in his pockets and strolling toward the intersection. He peered around the corner and paused, admiring the swing of her hips and the way her thick blonde hair bounced with each confident stride. It was just his luck the woman he'd been sent to investigate was the most gorgeous creature he'd ever seen.

During their brief encounter at the Halloween party a few nights ago, her stunning smile and contagious laugh had almost reeled him in. He would have gladly spent the night with her—but thank the gods he didn't—using their mutual attraction as a way into her house to investigate her crimes. *Would have.* Until she'd excused herself to the "restroom" and the weirdness had begun.

He followed her a few more blocks, pausing as she bent down to pet one of the dogs, scratching it behind the ears and flashing that breathtaking smile. *Damn.* The things he'd like to do with that woman...

But he was on a mission, damn it. He had to find his missing packmate and the witch who cursed his kind, and this exquisite blonde was the prime suspect. The only suspect. The head on his shoulders needed to have a come-to-Jesus meeting with the one in his pants, because he was *not* getting in bed with the enemy. Not again.

The evening sun began its descent behind the nine-teenth-century French Quarter buildings, painting the sky in shades of deep purple and orange, casting long shadows across the pavement still damp from the afternoon rain. A violinist played a classical tune on the corner of Royal Street, drawing a crowd, and Trace almost lost sight of the beautiful vixen.

His heart began to sprint, but as he rounded the corner, he found her on the front steps of a Creole townhouse, unleashing a boxer and patting it on its flank before it bolted inside. She wound up the leash, clipping it to a ring near the wrist strap of her dog-walking apparatus, and continued on her way.

Trace blew out a relieved breath and followed as she delivered the rest of the animals to their homes. He was pushing it staying this long in the Quarter. Hell, spending five minutes within a two-mile radius of the place was dangerous for a red wolf shifter these days.

Someone, and he was looking at the probable culprit, had cursed his pack, forcing them to shift at random times. Whatever form they happened to be in when the spell struck, their bodies seized, their vision tunneling as the magic forced them to shift.

A wild boar had nearly impaled Andy when he chased it too close to the city and was force-shifted mid-fight. He came to seconds before the tusk pierced his neck and then had to run home naked as a newborn.

Whatever magic she was using, it was sticky, and it

took a good half hour for it to wear off so they'd have control of their forms again.

Poor Becky was in bed with a human when the spell struck her. Imagine her date's surprise when the woman he was doing doggie style turned into an actual doggie. She'd had to enlist the help of a vampire to glamour the guy and make him forget he'd gotten lucky that night. Of course, he *was* lucky Becky didn't bite off his willy when she came to and found herself nose to nose with a shotgun. She'd made it out an open window before he had the chance to shoot, but that situation could have gone downhill fast.

The witch had to be stopped, and Trace was the werewolf to do it.

He followed her two more blocks, waiting on the sidewalk as she disappeared inside a coffee shop. Through the front window, he kept an eye on her as she chatted with the barista. She laughed, tossing her thick golden hair behind her shoulder, and as she turned, he caught a glimpse of the most radiant smile he'd ever seen.

His heart rate kicked up again, and he fisted his hands at his sides. He had to shake these unwelcome emotions stirring up his hormones. If the shit hit the fan between the red wolves and the witches, he did not want to get caught sheathing his sword in the enemy's scabbard.

Sophie rubbed the chill from the back of her neck as she waited for Crimson, her upstairs neighbor and owner of Evangeline's coffee shop, to finish mixing a weird concoction in a copper bowl. She'd had the strangest feeling that someone was watching her all afternoon, but every time she looked over her shoulder, no one seemed to be paying her any mind.

She'd been paranoid the past three days, ever since that damn werewolf bit her on Halloween and then took off without so much as an apology. Gaston still hadn't had any luck finding the bastard, but he assured her that if any of the wolfman's—or wolfwoman's—magic transferred to Sophie, they'd come looking for her to make sure she wasn't going to become one of them.

Her mind drifted to the delicious man she'd met that night before everything went to shit. Big and buff, with a full beard and thick, wavy hair, the guy was as close to a werewolf as she could imagine, and he looked like the perfect candidate to fulfill the palm reader's prophecy. Even if he couldn't have made her innermost dreams come true, she would've had a blast watching him try.

But her bladder had other plans for her that night, damn the bitch, and she'd lost him. She'd looked all over the club, but he'd vanished like the last homemade brownie at a church picnic. Disappointed that her awkwardness had once again lost her a potential date, she'd wandered into the courtyard and found what she'd thought was a dog cowering in the bushes.

It *so* wasn't a dog. She should have figured that out when it didn't calm down and take to her immediately. All animals loved her. All except werewolves, it seemed. She'd glimpsed yellow eyes and massive teeth as it snapped at her arm, and then it shot out of sight before she could get a good look at it.

So, she'd finally met a werewolf, but she still didn't know what one looked like. If this bite wound healed, she may never know. Hell, with the way things were going, it seemed she'd stay just as clueless about supes as the day Jane told her she'd become a vampire.

Sophie still couldn't get the witches in the tourist shops to give her a lick of information about their coven. Even when she showed them her grandma's grimoire, proving she was a descendant of a witch, they turned up their noses and directed her to the bookshelf if she wanted to learn about magic.

She watched the barista sprinkle a white powder into her bowl. Crimson was a witch. Sophie was sure of it, but she'd learned her lesson. They were becoming friends, and she wasn't mentioning magic until her neighbor brought it up.

Crimson's dark spiral curls bounced as she giggled and jumped, apparently pleased with whatever she'd been mixing. "Sorry about that."

She poured the mixture into a small glass bottle—a potion bottle for sure—and wiped her hands on a dishcloth. Her deep purple nails matched her satin shirt, a color that looked amazing against her dark brown skin tone. She wore skinny jeans with black ankle boots, and a gold rope belt accented her hoop earrings. The woman knew how to dress.

"Agrimony leaves have to be mixed when they're fresh, or they lose potency." She locked eyes with Sophie, suppressing a smile.

"What were you making?"

"It's an herbal remedy for a friend who isn't feeling like himself lately." The corners of her mouth twitched like she wanted to say more, and Sophie raised a brow, urging her to continue. Instead, Crimson inhaled deeply, two lines forming between her eyes as she cocked her head. "You smell different."

"I do?" Sophie sniffed her shoulder and then lifted her arm to smell her pit. She'd remembered to put on deodorant, so at least her friend wasn't reacting to BO.

"Yeah." Crimson leaned forward over the counter, inhaling again. "You've got a hint of a rustic, outdoorsy scent to you."

"I've been out walking dogs. Maybe that's what you smell?"

Crimson crossed her arms, drumming her fingers on her biceps. "Maybe. What do I smell like to you?"

Now there was a weird question. Well, weird for a human, which added more proof to Sophie's theory that the barista was a witch. "All I can smell is coffee."

"Really?" Crimson looked disappointed. If she was human, maybe she got a new perfume, and no one had noticed. Seriously, though, how could they over the rich, decadent scent of the best coffee in the South?

A black cat hopped onto the counter and let out a deep meow before rubbing against Sophie's arm.

"Hey there, handsome." Sophie ran a hand down the animal's back. "I didn't know you had a cat."

"Shoo, Jax. I told you to wait." Crimson chased the cat from the counter, and it sulked into the back room. "I've had him for a week or so. It's temporary. Like fostering, actually. He doesn't usually venture into the front like that. I'm not sure what's gotten into him."

"I have a way with animals." Sophie pushed up her sleeves. "Always have. Sometimes I could swear they understand me when I talk to them. Crazy, I know."

Crimson reached for a mug but paused. "That doesn't sound crazy. More like a gift."

"I've been thinking about getting a dog of my own. Taking care of other people's animals is fun, but it would be nice to have someone warm and loyal to come home to at the end of the day." She'd put off getting a pet in her younger years, when she was going out a lot and bringing random men home. Now that Jane was married, and Sophie's life had calmed down, she was itching for some stability. For somewhere to belong.

"Pets are a helluva lot easier than men, that's for sure." Crimson laughed then sucked in a quick breath, touching her fingers to her lips. "What happened to your arm?"

"Oh. A w…weird dog bit me. It's nothing." She jerked her sleeve down, clamping her mouth shut to keep the word "werewolf" from slipping out. Supes weren't too keen on their secrets getting around, and if whoever bit her did come looking for her, she didn't need them knowing she'd blabbed, even if it was to a probable witch.

Crimson glanced toward the doorway the cat disappeared through before leaning her forearms on the counter. "What did it look like?"

"I don't know. It was dark, and it ran off before I got a good look at it. A German shepherd, maybe?"

"Are you sure it was a dog?" Her dark eyes were intense, and Sophie almost gave in and told her what she knew. She wanted in with the witches of New Orleans so badly she could taste it, and Crimson was her ticket. She could feel it in her bones.

Instead, she simply shrugged. "Yeah. It's a little sore, but it'll heal. It hurt my pride more than anything. I started my dog walking business in college, and this is the first time I've ever been bitten."

"I thought you were new in town? You just moved in below me a few months ago."

"I started the company in Texas. I've got a manager running the business over there now, while I'm operating the new branch in New Orleans. I moved here to be with my bestie, but she works nights, so I don't get to see her as much as I'd like." Her bottom lip started to poke out, so she bit it. It wasn't Jane's fault she was dead to the world during daylight hours and would fry in the sunlight. The perks of being a vampire far outweighed the drawbacks, according to her best friend.

Crimson smiled. "Well, if you're ever in need of a friend to paint the town with, you know where I live."

"Thanks. I might take you up on that."

"I hope you do. Now, what can I get you?"

"The usual. A nonfat decaf vanilla latte."

"One *what's the point?* latte coming right up!" Crimson turned to the espresso machine, and Sophie laughed, tossing her hair behind her shoulder and glancing out the front window.

A man stared back at her, his dark honey eyes and auburn hair adding warmth to his tanned skin tone. He had a thick, well-groomed beard and a broad, muscular chest, and my, oh my, he looked like something she needed in her life. In fact, though it was hard to tell from the glare in the window, he looked an awful lot like the scrumptious man she lost in the club on Halloween.

"Hey, Crimson, hold off on the coffee. I may have found something else to warm me up tonight."

As her gaze locked with his, he jerked his head down and strode away, like he didn't mean for her to notice him. But honestly, how could she not? He was exactly the type of big, burly, alpha-looking man she'd been searching for.

The witch's smile slipped as her gaze locked with his through the glass, and her lips parted slightly. *Crap.* Trace ducked his head and paced up the sidewalk, the hairs on the back of his neck standing on end as he sensed her exiting the coffee shop.

Two more steps would have taken him to the corner, where he could disappear from her view, but the magic slammed into him like a frying pan to the face, knocking him mindless and sending him careening into a pothole the size of Lake Pontchartrain. Muddy water splashed around him as he shifted against his will, and he barely had time to shimmy out of his shirt before the entire world went dark.

"Oh, you poor little guy." The sweet voice danced in his ears, bringing him back to coherence.

He blinked his eyes open and found the blonde he'd been tailing hunched over him, biting her bottom lip and glancing up and down the street before returning her gaze to him. How long had he been out?

She offered him her hand, palm-down, holding it near his muzzle as if she expected him to sniff it. "Are you okay?"

Of course he wasn't okay. The witch had just forced him to shift in the middle of the street, and now his clothes lay beneath him, covered in mud, and he had to play the role of a house pet to avoid attracting any attention. Lucky for him, she'd made sure no witnesses were around, but damn she was bold performing magic in the open like that. He didn't know whether to admire her tenacity or bite her again.

He sniffed her hand, going along with the charade, a little whine emanating from his throat so she'd think he was scared.

Her smile brightened her sky-blue eyes. "That's a good boy. I thought I was losing my touch."

As she scratched his head, her sleeve slipped up to reveal the bandage on her forearm. A little pang of guilt shot through his chest before he reminded himself who she was and what she'd done to his pack. Her magic must have been animal-related, because his beast had been tamed at the first sound of her voice. Luckily, the man in him remained in control.

The sound of tires rolling on the pavement came from behind him, and Sophie looked up before rising to her feet. "Let's get you out of the road, okay, buddy? Can you stand?" She scratched under his chin, urging him to rise, and damn it if he didn't obey her command.

With her hand on the scruff of his neck, she guided him to the sidewalk as the car splashed through the pothole, ruining any chance he had at retrieving his clothes.

The witch knelt in front of him, taking his head in her hands, still pretending like she had nothing to do with his canine condition. "You're a mess, big guy. Do you have an owner around here anywhere?"

He blew out a hard breath through his nose. Was this woman serious? A witch knew better than to treat a werewolf like a house pet. Unless she thought her spell bound the man altogether... He might be able to use this to his advantage.

Her brow furrowed as she looked him over, running her hands along his neck and shoulders. "What are you? Some kind of German shepherd mix? You look a little bit like a coyote, but you're way too tame to be a wild animal."

Oh, he'd show her wild. As soon as he found his

missing friend, this witch would be wishing she never messed with the red wolf pack.

She glanced around the empty sidewalk and leaned toward his ear. "You're not a werewolf, are you? One of those bit me a few nights ago, and my arm's been throbbing ever since."

As if she didn't know. What game was this woman playing?

"You didn't happen to see a big guy with a sexy beard walk by a few minutes ago, did you?" She pursed her lips, shaking her head. "I should be so lucky." Rising to her feet, she rested her hands on her hips and gave him a curious look. "I'm probably going to regret this, but I think I'll take you home with me. We can get you cleaned up and then look online to see if anyone's missing you. What do you think?"

This could be his chance. If she took him into her home in wolf form, with his heightened senses, he'd be able to sniff out his missing packmate. Then, with Jackson's help, they could subdue her, powerful magic or not, and get her to lift the spell before his pack broke the truce with the witches and started a war.

He followed her back toward the coffee shop and into a side entrance of the building, where she stopped at the foot of a staircase.

She glanced up the steps and down at him, her eyes calculating. "What do you weigh, boy? About sixty or seventy pounds? I can't have you tracking mud through the place."

He backed up. Was she seriously considering carrying him?

Squatting, she scooped him into her arms and rose to

her feet, letting out a little grunt on the way up. "It's a good thing I work out," she said, her voice strained.

She struggled up the stairs, and Trace did his best to remain still, ignoring the humiliation of being carried. He wasn't about to ruin his chance at getting inside the enemy's lair.

She set him on the landing to tug a key from her pocket and open the door before scooping him up again and carrying him inside.

She marched through the living room, and he noted a door leading to a balcony as well as an archway that probably led to the kitchen. As they entered her bedroom, she made a sharp left straight into the bathroom, depositing him in the tub. A closet door stood closed against the far wall, but he didn't get a good enough look at the bedroom to determine any other openings that could lead to his friend.

He sat on his haunches, watching as she regarded her soiled shirt in the mirror. She frowned and sighed, and he started to feel a little bad for ruining her clothes. Evil witch or not, he couldn't deny the effect she had on him. His wolf wanted to please her. Hell, she'd have the beast rolling over and eating from her hand if the man didn't hold on to control.

She had a calming effect, which was why she was able to wrangle so many alphas on leashes earlier today. The man in him found her drop-dead gorgeous, which set off warning sirens in his mind. If he wasn't careful, she'd have both man and beast entranced with her magic, and he'd never accomplish his mission.

Turning on the water, she dropped to her knees beside the tub and grabbed a large plastic cup from a shelf. Holding her good wrist under the stream, she heated the water and then filled the cup, dumping the contents over his fur until he was sopping wet.

She squirted some flowery-smelling shampoo onto his back, and while he wanted to protest the girly scent, when her fingers dug into his coat, massaging him, he may as well have been a pile of putty on the floor. He didn't sense her using her powers, but her hands felt like magic.

He shouldn't have enjoyed it so much, but technically, he was doing his job. He'd penetrated the enemy's stronghold, but as she leaned into the tub to wash the mud from his paws, he caught a glimpse of flesh and satin down her shirt, and his mind immediately went to another form of penetration.

Damn, this woman was gorgeous. And the rustic scent of his magic mixing with the warm cinnamon fragrance of hers created an intoxicating aroma he wanted to wrap himself up in.

*Focus, Trace.* He shook his body, hoping to shake the intruding thoughts from his mind, and water flew everywhere, coating the blonde in suds and wetness.

"Hey, now. That was rude, mister," she scolded him, but an amused smile curved her lips as she spoke. "Let's get you rinsed so I can have a turn, okay?" She dumped cups of water over him, and the bubbles spiraled down the drain before she grabbed a fluffy towel and dried his fur. A man could get used to this kind of attention.

"A beautiful dog like you needs a name. Do you have one?" She held his face and stared into his eyes. "It's not Rover, is it? You'd be surprised how many people still call their dogs that."

He huffed to let her know his name was definitely not Rover, and she laughed. Staring into her blue eyes, he focused his thoughts, pushing his name toward her mind.

If she really was a witch with animal-controlling powers, she should pick up on the message. It would explain how the dogs she walked knew exactly where she wanted them to be.

She narrowed her eyes, pursing her lips. "I suppose I can give you a name."

He focused again, sending her his thoughts.

Her eyes widened. "For some weird reason, I want to call you Trace. It's not really a dog name, but it fits. What do you think?"

He licked her nose. Suspicion confirmed.

"Okay, okay. Come on." She gestured for him to get out of the tub, and his wolf obeyed before the man could even think about her request.

Picking up a hairdryer, she held it toward him. "This is going to make some noise, but it'll be warm, and it'll help you dry faster. Is it okay if I use this on you?"

He sniffed it like a good boy and was rewarded with another sweet smile. How could someone this kind and gentle with animals be responsible for the turmoil in his pack? It didn't make sense.

With his coat dry and fluffy, and shinier than it had ever been, she released him from the bathroom. He darted from room to room, sniffing the floor and furniture, using his snout to open doors and check out all the closets. Jackson wasn't here. In fact, even with his heightened sense of smell, he didn't detect a trace of magic. She must have performed her spells somewhere else.

Her gaze weighed on his shoulders, and he stopped, cocking his head at her as she stood in the doorway, leaning against the jamb with her arms crossed. "Are you done?"

He inched toward her and sat, trying his best to act like a domesticated dog.

She laughed and scratched behind his ears. "Don't mark your territory while I'm in the shower, okay?"

No worries about that. As soon as he accomplished his mission, he'd be getting as far away from this entrancing witch as he could. He jumped onto her bed, expecting her to protest, but she simply smiled again. After turning in a circle, he plopped onto the mattress and rested his head on his paws, his gaze trained on the bathroom door as she closed it behind her.

## CHAPTER THREE

Sophie cinched the towel around her chest and tousled her damp hair. Wiping the fog from the mirror, she stared at her reflection and sighed. A dog that sweet probably had an owner, and even if he didn't, he was too big to keep in an apartment.

Then again, if he got along with her clients, she could walk him three or four times a day. That should be enough exercise, shouldn't it? Lord knew she could use the companionship. Making friends proved difficult when she had one foot in the supernatural world and one in the human. She couldn't talk about Jane or Ethan, or even Gaston with humans, but she didn't fit in with the supes either. It was like high school all over again.

She ran her fingers over the bite mark on her arm, and the wound tingled. Thanks to her BFF's magical spit, it was healing nicely, but as much as she was averse to sprouting fur, she almost wished she'd turn into a werewolf so she'd belong somewhere. She'd prefer a coven, but being part of a pack might be nice.

In the meantime, she could make her own pack. As

long as Trace didn't have an owner out there looking for him, the dog would stay.

She grabbed her lavender-scented deodorant from the shelf, and her vision tunneled. Her head spun, and she squeezed her eyes shut, steadying herself with a hand on the edge of the sink. "Whoa. I shouldn't have skipped lunch."

As she shook her head, the fogginess dissipated, the lightheaded sensation ceasing as quickly as it had begun. She lifted her arm to apply her deodorant, and instead of finding her smooth, freshly-shaven pit, a patch of tan hair occupied the space under her arm.

"What the hell?" She examined it in the mirror, running her finger over the soft strands. *Holy shit.* That wasn't hair. It was fur. A freaking tuft of fur had sprouted in her pit like one of those carpet sample squares on display at Home Depot. She lifted the other arm, and that pit was furry too.

"Oh, no," she whispered to her reflection. "I said I *almost* wished I'd turn into a werewolf. I don't really want to." Snatching the razor from its hook in the shower, she shaved the patches of fur, collecting the strands in the sink before wrapping them in a piece of toilet paper.

Maybe it was a side effect of the bite. Maybe once it healed, this problem would go away. *Please let it go away.* She stuffed the fur wrapped in toilet paper into the medicine cabinet and closed the mirrored door. Jane would be there soon, and she'd know what to do. Her BFF always had a plan. In less than a year of being undead, Jane had managed to befriend the vampire Magistrate, the highest-ranking bloodsucker in the state. Surely she could find out what the hell was happening with Sophie's body and how to stop it. Supes were supes, and while they didn't share their secrets, they all knew each other. Jane could get her in contact with someone who could help.

Biting her lip, she hesitated to lift her arms again. If the fur had already grown back, she'd have to splurge on laser hair removal at the local medspa.

*Oh no.* What if, since she was only part witch, this werewolf gig was only going to affect her underarms? Would lasers even work to remove magic-induced fur?

Squeezing her eyes shut, she raised her arms above her head and held her breath. She opened one eye, then the other, and a gush of air made her cheeks puff as she exhaled her relief. For the time being, at least, she was fur-free.

As she opened the bathroom door, a cloud of steam wafted into the bedroom. She stepped from the tile to the carpet and froze. As if her armpit ordeal wasn't enough, there, lying on his side, his knees pulled to his chest, was not the fluffy, rust-colored dog she'd brought home. It was a tall, muscular, totally naked man.

"Ah!" She dove for the pepper spray in her nightstand drawer. Holding it in her right hand as threateningly as possible, she rocked from foot to foot, her mind scrambling to catch up with what was happening. "Who are you? What have you done with my dog?"

"Huh?" The man blinked his eyes open and glanced around, disoriented. He held his hands in front of his face and groaned. "Oh, shit." He slid off the mattress, putting the bed between them, and rose to his feet, his hands lifted in surrender.

"Who are you?" She waved her weapon, trying to hold a fierce expression as recognition dawned in her mind. She knew exactly who this guy was. "How did you get in here? Where's my dog?"

She tried to hold eye contact, but her gaze kept dropping against her will. He had a broad chest with a sprinkling of auburn hair that trailed down the middle of chiseled abs, leading right to his… *Oh my.* Even flaccid, the man was hung.

"My eyes are up here, sweetheart." He had a deep, rumbly voice that melted as smooth as Velveeta in her ears.

"You…" She looked into the deep honey-brown of his irises, but her gaze dipped below his waist again, her eyeballs completely ignoring the command from her brain.

He chuckled and held a pillow in front of himself. "Better?"

"No, now your dick is on my pillow. I lay my head there at night, you know." She waved her weapon again, and he laughed.

"Would you rather I put my dick somewhere else?" Mischief danced in his eyes, and she tried to ignore the flutter in her belly.

"Are you hitting on me? First you disappear on me at the club, then you stalk me at the coffee shop. You break into my house, climb into my bed buck naked while I'm in the shower, and *now* you're hitting on me?"

"You're the one waving a dildo around. Who's hitting on whom?"

Her eyes widened as she realized she did, in fact, have the vibrator she'd affectionately named Big Blue in her hand. "Dammit." She snatched the actual can of pepper spray from the drawer and held it toward him. "Don't come near me. What did you do with Trace?"

"I *am* Trace."

"Don't try to be funny, mister. If you hurt that dog, I'll…"

He arched a brow. "You know exactly what I am, so stop pretending. Where's Jackson?"

"Pretending? You're the delusional one, breaking into my apartment, rubbing your man bits all over my bed like a…" Her mouth fell open as the voice in the back of her head began shouting. "Like a dog." She lowered the vibrator and the pepper spray, but kept them clutched tightly just in case. "You're a werewolf?"

"As if you didn't know."

"But…you're so small."

He frowned and held the pillow tighter against his groin. "It's cold in here, and you're threatening to beat me with pepper spray and a dildo. What do you expect?"

She dropped the vibrator into the drawer. Big Blue was a lover, not a fighter. "I meant your wolf. I thought you were some kind of German shepherd mix. Aren't were-wolves supposed to be gigantic? They are in *Twilight*."

He grunted. "Don't even mention that movie. Anyway, I'm a red wolf. We're smaller than our gray cousins, but we're no less fierce."

The pillow slipped down so she could see the tuft of hair right above his dick, and her tongue involuntarily slipped out to moisten her lips. Damn her body and its inappropriate reactions to finding a strange man in her bed. "Where are your clothes?"

He pulled up the pillow. "Probably still in the muddy pothole where you forced me to shift."

"What on earth are you talking about? Here." She ducked into the bathroom and grabbed a towel from a shelf, tossing it to him. "Put that on at least."

He dropped the pillow on the bed, completely

unashamed—honestly, the man had absolutely nothing to be ashamed about—and wrapped the towel around his waist.

Sophie swallowed hard, willing her brain to catch up. "What do you mean I forced you to shift? I didn't even know you were a man." With his bottom half covered, she finally focused on his face. "Why were you following me?"

"You're the witch who kidnapped my friend and cursed my pack." He crossed his arms.

"I did no such thing, and I'm not a witch."

"I can smell the magic on you."

"Oh, really?" She mirrored his posture, still clutching the pepper spray. "What does it smell like?"

"Cinnamon and cider. Warm." He inhaled deeply. "Delicious." His eyes flashed as if he hadn't meant to say the last part.

That's exactly what the vampires said she smelled like, but she still didn't have any powers. The bite mark throbbed from clutching her arms so tightly, so she dropped them to her sides.

He looked at the wound and winced. "Have you started exhibiting any canine attributes? Growing fur in strange places or craving raw meat?"

"Ew. No." Raw meat? She would never. "You're the one who bit me, aren't you? Gaston said you'd come looking for me. What? You can't find a mate on your own, so you thought you'd turn a human?" Okay, maybe that was a little harsh, but the man had been stalking her.

His jaw clenched. "If I wanted you as my mate, you'd come to me willingly, sweetheart."

"Oh, you're sure of yourself, aren't you? How do you know I'm even interested in men?"

He chuckled, shaking his head. "Your pupils are

dilated, for one thing, and you can't keep your eyes off my dick."

She gasped, trying to act offended, but the guy had a point. She may have turned into a bumbling idiot every time she tried to flirt, but she couldn't deny the attraction.

"And your hormones make your scent stronger. The whole room smells like wassail and gingerbread cookies, and I can only imagine it's because you like what you see." He swept a heated gaze down her body. "The view's nice from my end too, by the way."

Her mouth opened and closed a few times as she tried to gather her thoughts. This naked werewolf was making some pretty heavy accusations—kidnapping, cursing—yet all she could think about was yanking that towel from around his waist and seeing what his package looked like fully extended. *Get a grip, Soph.*

"So why did you bite me? It was pretty shitty of you to run off, too. You could have at least apologized."

He started to answer, but the doorbell rang, and she held up a finger. *Finally.* "That'll be Jane. She'll be able to sort this mess out. Wait here."

Sophie padded to the living room and opened the door. "Hey, girl. You're just in time."

Jane's dark eyes took in Sophie's state of undress before she peered over her shoulder. "Just in time for what? I'm not having a three-way." She leaned closer and whispered, "When were you going to tell me you finally found your werewolf? He's cute. Do you want me to come back tomorrow?"

"Trace!" Sophie whirled to face him. "I told you to stay in the bedroom."

He crossed his arms over his chest, his biceps bunching as they contracted, looking sexy as hell and doing it on purpose. "You may be able to control animals with your mind, but the *man* is in control of this werewolf."

"Why's he talking about controlling animals?" Jane strutted in and perched on the arm of the sofa.

"He's accusing me of kidnapping his friend and putting a curse on his pack. Something about forcing them to shift. I don't know." Sophie threw her arms in the air. "Will you watch him while I get dressed?"

"Shouldn't you both put on some clothes?" Jane swept her gaze over Trace, nodding her approval. "Or not."

"He came here naked."

Jane's eyes widened.

"I was in wolf form when she supposedly mistook me for a dog and brought me inside. My clothes are in a muddy pothole on Royal Street." He turned to Sophie. "This doesn't have to be difficult. Just tell me where Jackson is, lift the curse, and we'll be on our way. I won't tell the witches what you did; my pack won't start a war, no harm done."

Sophie looked at Jane with pleading eyes. Luckily, that was all it took for her BFF to take action.

"Go get dressed." Jane tugged her phone from her pocket. "I'll call Ethan and get him and Gaston to come. This is way over my head." She looked at Trace. "What are you? About a 34/36?"

He nodded. "How'd you know?"

"I worked retail for a little while."

Sophie marched into her bedroom and tossed her pepper spray in the drawer. Trace didn't seem like a threat, and even if he were, he'd be no match for a bunch of vampires. She threw on some skinny jeans and a lowcut sweater. Even if the guy was accusing her of crimes she couldn't possibly commit, he was hot as sin. No harm in flaunting her physical gifts, including the rack she spent four grand on.

She returned to the living room to find Jane chatting with the intruder like they were old friends. "Did you know Trace is a police officer? A werewolf and a man in uniform. You hit the jackpot."

"I'm taking a leave of absence from my job until the culprit is apprehended," he said.

So his outfit at the Halloween party wasn't a costume. He was a real cop. His ranking on the sexy scale just tipped over the edge. "Too bad he thinks I'm the culprit." Sophie sank into the recliner and crossed her legs, grinning as Trace's gaze landed on her chest. Her pupils weren't the only ones dilating. *Take that, Mr. Sexy Wolfman.*

"Can y'all explain this from the beginning?" Jane asked. "These bits and pieces you're throwing at me aren't making any sense."

"He pretended to be a dog so I'd bring him inside my apartment. While I was in the shower, he turned back human and started throwing accusations like spaghetti, seeing what he could make stick."

"I wasn't pretending anything. You forced me to shift."

"Hold on, both of you." Jane held up her hands. "Back it up all the way. Trace, I think you have details we're missing."

He narrowed his eyes at Sophie for a moment before focusing on Jane. "A little over a week ago, Jackson Altuve went missing from the pack. I talked to him that afternoon, and he told me he was hooking up with a witch. No one has seen him since."

"Okay," Jane said. "Now we're getting somewhere. Soph, did you go out with Jackson?"

She scoffed. "No! Whose side are you on?"

"I'm just trying to get all the facts. Trace, why do you think Sophie is responsible for Jackson's disappearance?"

"Because our Alpha met with the coven's high priestess. She questioned every registered witch in the French Quarter, under oath. They all denied it."

"Well, someone obviously lied," Sophie said.

"And risk having her magic bound for life?" Trace shook his head. "No witch in her right mind would take that chance. The coven values honesty and truth. They don't take lightly to liars."

Another knock sounded on the door, and Ethan and Gaston strolled in. Ethan's face was serious, like always, and he said something to Jane in her mind because she smiled and nodded, taking the clothes he offered her and handing them to Trace.

Must be nice to have all those special powers. All Sophie had was a yummy scent only supes could smell and furry armpits.

She introduced the vampires to the werewolf...*will this ever feel normal?*...and Trace disappeared into the bedroom to finally put some clothes on as she and Jane updated the guys on his story.

Gaston laughed. "He thinks you're responsible for cursing his pack?"

"She's the only unregistered witch in the Quarter whose magic hasn't been tested. She has to be responsible." Trace stood at the living room entrance wearing faded jeans and a gray t-shirt that hugged his muscular chest. *Woof.*

"I can assure you, wolf, that Miss Sophie had nothing

to do with a curse on your pack." Gaston rested his elbows on the arms of the chair. "She has no magical powers. You can see that in her aura."

"She's hiding them. I can smell the magic on her." He sauntered into the room and offered his hand to Ethan. "Thank you for the clothes. I'll pay you back when I find my wallet."

"No problem." Ethan rested a hand on Jane's knee. "Tell us about the curse. Someone is forcing you to shift?"

"It started on Halloween night. I was at your party, keeping tabs on Sophie, when her magic slammed into me like a baseball bat to my skull. I managed to stumble into the courtyard before I shifted and blacked out. When I woke up, I hid my uniform in the brush because I couldn't shift back."

"So you bit me because you thought I made you shift?" *Unbelievable.* It figured her first werewolf would be the *bite first, ask questions later* type.

"I hid in the bushes when you came out, and when you found me, your magic subdued my wolf. He wanted to roll over and let you scratch his belly, but I held him back. I was trying to run, but you kept reaching for me. My wolf wanted to go to you; I wanted to bolt. The signals got crossed, and I accidentally bit. I didn't mean to, and I'm sorry for that."

"Well." She crossed her arms, lifting her chin defiantly. "Thank you for finally apologizing, but I did not make you shift, and I don't know your friend. You're the first werewolf I've ever met, and like Gaston said, I don't have any powers. My grandmother was a witch, and that's what you smell. Believe me, the witches don't want me in their coven. I've tried. Now." She stood and dusted imaginary lint from her jeans. This was all too much to process, and with her hormones battling for control of her brain, it was best if Trace was far, far away. "I'd like you to leave. I've had about all I can take tonight."

Trace glanced at the vampires as if weighing his options, but honestly, what more could he do? He couldn't prove Sophie had anything to do with his friend or his pack problems, because she didn't. It was his word against hers, and she had three badass vampires backing her up.

With a heavy sigh, he stood and shuffled toward the door. "Do you have a pen and paper, so I can leave you my number?" He gestured to her arm. "If anything happens with the bite, we'll need to take care of you."

Take care of her how? By nurturing her or by taking her out? "Nothing's going to happen with it. It's healing just fine."

"Please? For my peace of mind."

"Fine." Anything to get him out the door. It wasn't like she actually had to call the man. She marched to the kitchen and grabbed a pen and a Post-It note.

He scribbled his name and two phone numbers on the yellow sheet. "The second one is my landline, just in case something happens before I get a new phone. I'm sure my old one is toast."

"I'd say I'm sorry, but I'm not the one who made you shift. And if you hadn't been stalking me, you wouldn't have been in the street to begin with."

With a sardonic chuckle, he straightened his spine and opened the door. "I'm sorry we didn't meet under different circumstances, Sophie. Your bed is comfortable." He winked and slipped out the door.

She clenched her teeth, angry, not at him, but at herself for the stupid flutter in her belly his comment caused. She should have been offended. Hell, a normal woman would have at least been a little scared of a big, burly, dominant guy like Trace, but all Sophie could think about was the shape of his body, the cut of his muscles, and all the things she'd like to do with his dick.

"This is an interesting event turning." Gaston rose to his feet, his eyes glinting with his devilish smile. "I told you you'd be better off with a vampire."

"It's *turn of events*, and I've told you cold and dead is not my type."

"Undead." Gaston smirked. "There's quite a difference, *ma chère*." He winked, and Sophie wanted to laugh, but the gravity of the situation weighed her down.

"Can you guys excuse us for a second? I need to talk to Jane privately."

Gaston bowed. "We'll be right outside the door."

Jane looked at Ethan. "Take him down the street. This is girl stuff."

"Got it." Ethan escorted Gaston out of the apartment, and Sophie motioned for Jane to follow her to the bathroom.

"Promise you won't tell anyone what I'm about to show you?" Sophie held up her hand, and Jane linked her pinky finger with hers.

"On my life."

Sophie tilted her head.

Jane sighed. "On my *undead* life. What's going on? You're on the pill, aren't you? Did he hurt you? Does he have a disease?"

"No, he didn't touch me, and yes, of course I'm on the pill. Look at this." She pulled the toilet paper bundle from the medicine cabinet and unwrapped the contents.

Jane peered at her hand. "What is that?"

"It's fur, Jane. Fucking fur."

CHAPTER FOUR

"You were in her house, and you found nothing?" Teresa shook her head, unbelieving.

"Not a thing." Trace glanced into the Alpha's eyes before lowering his gaze, showing respect to the woman in charge of his pack. "No trace of Jackson and not even a splash of magic."

His back ramrod straight, he clasped his hands in his lap and glanced at the portraits on the wall. Three Alphas, all men, stared back, their judgmental gazes boring into him, making him sweat. Teresa was the first female Alpha in the history of his pack, sworn in fifty years ago after a war with the neighboring gray wolves cut the red wolf population in half.

The office, an expansive room in the Alpha's two-story cabin in the woods, boasted rustic hardwood floors and brick-lined walls. A massive oak desk took up a quarter of the space, and Trace sat in the center of a line of seven wooden chairs facing it.

Teresa wore her dark brown hair pulled back in a tight

bun, and she crossed her arms, the vinyl office chair squeaking as she leaned back and narrowed her eyes skeptically. "Did you look, or were you too busy dipping your pen in the enemy's inkwell?"

He blinked once, refusing to flinch at the verbal slap in the face. "No, ma'am. I didn't lay a finger on the witch. I went in with the mission, and only the mission, in mind." Maybe that was stretching the truth a little, but his attraction to Sophie didn't matter as long as his actions reflected the pack's interest in her and not his own.

The witch was beautiful, kind, caring, great with animals. And she wasn't the slightest bit embarrassed when he called her out for trying to defend herself with a vibrator, which hinted at how adventurous she might be in the sack. His lips attempted to curve into a smile, but he fought the urge, keeping his expression neutral. If the Alpha knew his real feelings for Sophie, he'd be off this case quicker than a vampire could down a pint of blood.

"This is your chance to redeem yourself," she said. "To prove you still deserve to be my First Lieutenant."

"I know." He clenched his teeth, trying to keep his mind out of Sophie's bedroom.

"Jackson is your best friend."

"Yes, ma'am. I won't screw it up."

Ever since that wood nymph who'd hidden all the prey animals from his pack seduced him, he'd been busting his ass to prove he still deserved to be the Alpha's second. In his defense, she had put him under a spell. He didn't know his snout from his tail when he was around the nymph, and Teresa herself had come in to save him and chase the creature away.

The minute the nymph left New Orleans, the spell was

broken, and Trace could think straight again, but he'd been wary of anyone with magical powers ever since.

He should have been wary of the witch. He was until he woke up naked in her bed. Her stunned reaction wasn't fake, and he couldn't fathom a reason why she'd force-shift him back to human in the first place. Her magic centered around animals, so she wouldn't have given up control. Something didn't add up.

"Do you want me to make another appointment with the high priestess?" he asked. "Maybe they missed a witch during the questioning."

"Don't you dare. Our relations with the coven are already on edge. They held up their end of the truce by questioning everyone under oath. The culprit is unregistered, untested, and there's only one untested witch in the French Quarter."

"I don't think Sophie is responsible. She doesn't seem capable—"

"Like that nymph didn't seem capable of setting up a magical barrier to keep all the prey out of our hunting grounds?"

"That was different," he grumbled, sounding more like a pouting child than a grown-ass man. *Get yourself together. You're acting like a scolded pup.*

"Was it different?" She rose to her feet and paced behind her desk. "She has *vampires* vouching for her. Why not witches? The coven is convinced she's not a threat, but I'm not. She's hiding something, and you need to find out what."

"How would you like me to proceed?"

"I need someone to get close to her. Befriend her and her vampire allies. Can I trust you with the job, or should I send in one of the new recruits?"

His hackles rose. Trace was the pack's First Lieutenant. It was his job to handle situations like this, not some fledgling working his way up the ranks. "You can count on me, Alpha. I learn from my mistakes."

"Good. The French Quarter is still under quarantine, so spend as little time there as possible. I expect a report in three days, if not sooner."

"Yes, ma'am. I won't let you down." He turned to leave.

"Trace." She fixed him with a serious gaze. "She's not part of the coven, so the truce doesn't apply. Once you find Jackson, you're authorized to use any means necessary to end her magic."

Pressing his lips into a hard line, he nodded once and stepped out the door. As soon as it clicked shut, he leaned against the wall and closed his eyes. Teresa's *any means necessary* line was a silent order, one he'd be obliged to obey under different circumstances. But the Alpha didn't know he'd already screwed up this mission by biting Sophie. She could be one of them by the end of the month, and then what? Taking out their own kind was illegal.

Red wolves had dwindled in numbers nearly to the point of extinction. Their non-shifting cousins hadn't been spotted in Louisiana in years, and Trace's pack, though strong, was one of the smallest in the country. If Sophie did become a shifter, and she mated within the pack...

He ground his teeth. The witch was the enemy. No matter how hot a fire she lit in his core, he had to remember his mission, and his mission did *not* include getting Sophie into bed and especially not claiming her as his mate. His attraction to her was clouding his judgment, and that ended now.

Straightening his spine, he marched out of the Alpha's cabin and into the forest. He'd have to take care of this before the next full moon. There was no way around it.

---

"You were such a good boy today, Ruger." Sophie sat on a concrete block outside the entrance to Louis Armstrong Park to rest her aching feet and scratched the Boston terrier behind the ears. "I'll have to let your dad know to give you some extra treats tonight."

She peered across Rampart, the divided street on the outskirts of the French Quarter, and smiled as a little girl waved from the window of a passing streetcar. Ruger's home, an orange two-story Creole cottage, stood across the intersection, with a divided shotgun home on one side and an expansive three-story brick hotel on the other.

A man with a fluffy chocolate Pomeranian walked by, making Ruger's ears perk up. Sophie rested a hand on the Boston terrier's back, and he sat still as the Pom trotted toward them, sniffing Sophie's ankles.

She tried to say hello to the man, but her brain couldn't decide whether *hi* or *good morning* was appropriate, so it came out as, "Hide 'orning."

"Hello." The man tilted his head, flashing a hesitant smile before tugging his dog down the street.

Sophie sighed, and as she straightened her spine, rotating her ankles to loosen the tension, a wave of dizziness washed over her. The edges of her vision darkened, her entire body shuddering—no, shaking—like a wet dog trying to dry its coat.

She gasped, and, glancing up and down the street to be sure she hadn't attracted any attention, she slipped her hand through the neck of her shirt to feel her armpit. *Whew. Fur-free.* That full-body shudder was the werewolf magic leaving her system. *Yeah, that's what it was.*

Ruger made a whining sound in his throat, and as she reached down to comfort him, the dog latched onto her leg and started going to town on her shin like it was his personal plaything.

"Ew! Ruger, no. Bad dog." She pried the terrier from her leg, but the moment she set him on the concrete, he went at it again, moving his little hips like he was the Energizer Bunny with a fresh set of batteries.

"Ugh!" She stood, yanking her leg from Ruger's love grip as she tightened his leash, holding him at arm's length and marching across the intersection. "What's gotten into you?" He pranced and bounced, excited as all get-out, until she shoved him through his front door and locked him in his house.

With her morning round complete, she plopped onto Ruger's front steps and checked her phone. Three new inquiries for dog walking had come in overnight. Add those to the six on the waiting list, and it was time she hired some help. She might even look into renting an office space if this branch was going to get as big as her Austin home base.

Business was finally starting to take off, and Sophie was looking at possibly turning into a dog herself. *Fan-friggin-tastic.* She shoved her phone in her pocket and rose to her feet. If all the dogs started acting like this little guy just did, she'd be in a mess of trouble.

Of course, that big, sexy wolfman she found in her bed yesterday evening could probably help her figure out what the hell was going on, but then she'd have to admit she needed his assistance. After the way he snuck in, let her *bathe* him—she gave the man a friggin' bath for Christ's sake—and then accused her of all that crap, she wasn't about to ask him for help. He could go hump a light pole for all she cared.

She was *not* going to turn into a werewolf anyway. There simply wasn't enough magic running through her veins for it to happen, and she would keep telling herself that until the next full moon came and went, leaving her the same old awkward, boring human she'd always been.

Pushing the thoughts out of her mind, she focused on the current dilemma. Coffee or lunch? She'd hardly slept last night. Images of Trace in all his glorious nakedness danced behind her eyes every time she closed them. She'd had so many sexy dreams about the man, she had to break out Big Blue this morning just to cool herself off.

And there she was, getting all hot and bothered again. She shook her head. Coffee. Crimson's shop stood a block away, so she'd stop in for a double-shot latté and then grab some lunch.

Crimson leaned in the doorway of Evangeline's, chatting with a tall, slim guy in his early twenties. With short black hair and dark brown eyes, he was cute, but still a little lanky for Sophie's taste. Put another ten years on him, when his shoulders had filled out and a little stubble peppered his jaw, and he might have been hot. Not that it mattered what the man looked like. Sophie was just desperate for a distraction. Anything to get her mind off werewolves.

Aside from the too-young-to-be-hot man, several dozen paintings occupied the sidewalk in front of the café. Done in deep, vibrant hues, the canvases depicted cartoonish renderings of houses and famous landmarks throughout the French Quarter. A twenty by thirty-inch swamp landscape stood on an easel by the door, and Sophie stopped to admire the vivid artistry.

"I'll make you a deal on that one, since we're friends." Crimson strutted toward her. She wore knee-high boots with three-inch heels, easily putting her at six feet tall. "Three hundred, and it's yours."

"Are you nuts?" the man asked. "That one's worth at least five hundred."

"Sophie." Crimson draped an arm around her shoulders. "I'd like you to meet my baby brother, Josh."

"Hi." Sophie shook his hand and glanced at Crimson. "Your brother?"

She nodded. "When Josh isn't trying to make people pay too much for paintings once a month at my café, he's studying art history in grad school."

"Five hundred is reasonable for an original painting that size," he said. "I won't take less."

"An artist knows the value of his work better than anyone," Sophie said, leaning closer and admiring the exquisite detail of the piece. "If I had a wall big enough to put it on, I'd buy it."

Crossing her arms, Crimson smirked at her brother. "And she'd pay three hundred because the artist knows the value of *her* work better than anyone."

Sophie's eyes widened. "You painted all these?"

"I sure did. I have dozens more in my apartment too. You'll have to come up and see them sometime." She motioned for her to follow and disappeared through the café door.

"It was nice to meet you, Josh." Sophie nodded and followed Crimson inside the empty shop.

"You want the usual?" Crimson stepped behind the counter and tied an apron around her waist.

"Full caffeine. Make it a double shot. I didn't sleep much last night." She slid onto a stool at the counter.

Crimson arched a brow. "Because you were having too much fun, I hope?"

"I wish." She leaned her forearms on the counter, drumming her chipped lavender nails against the Formica. She was way overdue for a manicure. "Your paintings are beautiful. Why do you run a coffee shop instead of focusing on your art?"

"Art doesn't provide a steady income. Anyway, my mom used to own this place. I'm keeping it open in her honor."

"That's nice. How long ago did she pass?"

Crimson's laugh mixed with the sound of milk being steamed. "Oh, honey, she's not dead. My parents retired to Florida five years ago. Evangeline's is a mainstay in the French Quarter, so I promised to keep it running. Josh is supposed to be helping, but he decided he needed to go to grad school instead." She set the mug of vanilla latté in front of Sophie.

"Have you lived here all your life?"

"Since my parents adopted me when I was seven. What about you? Born and raised in Texas?"

Sophie sipped the coffee, closing her eyes for a moment to savor the rich vanilla flavor. "I'm an Army brat. We lived all over the world until my dad got a medical discharge when I was sixteen. That's when we moved to Texas, but even then, we went from Houston to Dallas to Austin in a year and a half. I haven't really belonged anywhere my entire life."

Crimson cocked her head, smiling warmly. "Well, welcome home."

The cat darted into the kitchen from a back room and leapt onto the countertop. Lifting its nose in the air, it sniffed twice before slinking toward Sophie and rubbing its head against her forearm. A deep purr rumbled in the cat's chest, and it stood on its back legs, resting its front paws on Sophie's shoulder, rubbing its head against her chin.

Sophie laughed, her heart melting. "Hey there, handsome. It's good to see you too." She really needed to get a pet of her own.

"Jeez." Crimson glared at the cat. "I know what we have is temporary, but could you at least *try* not to flirt with other women in front of me? Shoo. Go on in the back." She waved an arm, and the cat sulked toward the back room.

"He's fine. I don't mind the attention," Sophie said.

Crimson gave her a skeptical look. "Did he say anything to you?"

"He said you're feeding him too much salmon. He prefers beef." Crimson's eyes widened, and Sophie laughed. "I'm kidding. I don't understand animal speak."

"Hmm…" She pressed her lips together as if stopping herself from saying more. Because she *knew* more. Sophie was sure of it.

It was time she did a little gentle prying with her witch friend. Tracing her finger along the cool countertop, she chewed her bottom lip and chose her words carefully. "Yesterday, when you mentioned my fondness for animals being a gift, what did you mean by that?"

Crimson paused, searching her eyes and resting her hands on her hips. "You really don't know, do you?"

"Know what?"

She clasped her hand on Sophie's arm, closing her eyes and taking two deep breaths. Her lids fluttered open, and she shook her head, unbelieving. "All this time I thought you were hiding your powers, but they've never been unbound."

"Could you be a little less cryptic? I have no idea what you're talking about."

A slow smile curved Crimson's lips, and she glanced about the empty café, checking over her shoulder toward the door the cat disappeared through. "You have an ancestor who was a witch." She whispered the last word. "Do you know who it was? Mom? Grandma?"

A thrill shot up Sophie's spine as she straightened and leaned toward her. "My grandmother was. She died when my dad was little."

"That makes sense." Crimson nodded. "And your mom?"

Sophie shrugged. "She was as surprised as the rest of us when we found Gram's grimoire in the attic after Pop died."

"You have her grimoire?" Excitement buzzed around Crimson, her dark eyes gleaming. "Do you have it here, in New Orleans?"

"I do, but it doesn't work. I've tried a few of her spells, but nothing ever happens."

"Because your powers were never unbound." Resting her hands on the counter, she leaned toward her. "Sophie, you're a witch."

Sophie snorted. "Yeah, right. I've tried talking to every witch in the city about their coven, but they all just shut me down and point me to the bookshelf."

Crimson waved a hand dismissively. "You can't get

into the coven unless you're sponsored by another witch. I guarantee the high priestess has checked you out and determined you were harmless with bound powers. Most people this happens to go their entire lives thinking they're human."

"Hold on. Slow down." This was too much to process. In less than a year's time, her BFF became a vampire, married a vampire, and opened a vampire night club. The hottest man in New Orleans wound up in her bed as a werewolf, and now… "You're telling me I'm a witch? Like a full-blown magical being? Spells and incantations and sparkles and shit?"

"Well, you're not going to shoot glitter out your ass, but you are a witch." Crimson took off her apron and sashayed around the counter, parking on a stool next to Sophie. "Witches are born with their powers bound. It's up to the magical being who passed on those powers to unlock them when they're ready to begin training. If your grandma died when your dad was young, she took all that knowledge with her, and you've been living as a human ever since."

"Wow." She blinked.

"I know, right? My guess is your ability to talk to animals is your inborn gift. All witches can cast spells, but some of us are born with special psychic abilities: premonitions, talking to the dead, psychometry."

"Of all the cool powers I could have inherited, all I can do is talk to animals. That sounds about right."

"Maybe if your powers weren't bound, they could talk to you. I think you're a fauna witch." Her eyes gleamed, her smile brightening her entire face.

"Is there any way to unbind my powers?" Then again,

maybe the binding was the only thing keeping her from sprouting fur and howling at the moon. Would she still be a witch if she turned into a werewolf? Did were/witch hybrids even exist?

Crimson's face turned serious. "I think we might be able to help each other." She yanked a strand of hair from Sophie's head.

"Ow! I'm not even sure I want to have magical powers, though. I need some time to think about all this." Did those words really just leave her lips? Being a witch had consumed her thoughts ever since she found her grandma's grimoire, and now she was second-guessing herself?

"I may need a little more." Crimson yanked on another strand of hair.

"What do you need my hair for?" She rubbed her sore scalp.

"Divination." She wrapped the strands in a napkin and shoved them into her pocket before prancing around the counter. "Come by my apartment tonight around eight, and we'll talk. Bring the grimoire with you."

"You're not going to do anything to me before then?" Sophie gathered her hair into her hands, sweeping it over her shoulder, away from Crimson. "I don't want to be walking down the street and have magical sparkles explode out of my pores…or my ass."

The door chimed behind her, and a group of tourists entered the shop. "Hi, y'all. Welcome." Crimson waved a hand at the customers before leaning toward Sophie and lowering her voice. "I'm just going to read your energy. Now, shoo. No more witch talk around the humans." She gave her a conspiratorial wink before grabbing a tray of pastry samples and sashaying toward the customers.

Sophie grinned, excitement bubbling in her chest like champagne as she strode out the door. Sure, the fact she might have magical powers that could be unlocked was cool, but that wink from Crimson meant so much more. It meant there was a chance, however slim, that she could join the coven. That she might *belong*.

CHAPTER FIVE

Find Jackson. Stop the witch. They would have been
simple enough orders if the witch in question hadn't
been on his mind since the moment he saw her wrapped
in a towel, waving a dildo around like a sword.

A slow smile curved Trace's lips. He could show her a
sword. She'd never need that puny contraption again if he
warmed her bed every night. *Damn it.* He clenched his
fists as he stalked up Royal Street, following her scent.
*Focus on the plan.*

He passed two- and three-story structures in shades of
burgundy, yellow, and mauve as Sophie's entrancing,
magical fragrance grew stronger. Vibrant ferns and colorful
flowers adorned the galleries trimmed in decorative
wrought iron, and American, Spanish, French, and
Rainbow flags flapped in the cool November breeze.

Trace stuck close to the buildings, scanning the structures for the gates blocking the alley entrances. The magic
had struck him enough times now that he could sense the
force-shift before it happened. He should have time to

scale a gate and hide somewhere secluded if he felt it coming on.

So far, so good.

With his gaze locked on a dark green wooden gate across the street, he made a sharp right onto St. Philip, and a body smacked into him. She bounced off his chest, and he caught a whiff of her intoxicating cinnamon and cider scent before she landed on her ass in front of him.

Sophie wore black leggings that hugged her curves and a deep blue sweater with strands of silver woven through the fabric that caught the sunlight in sparkles, almost making her shimmer. Her golden hair had fallen across her face, and as she swept it behind her shoulders, her sky-blue eyes locked with his, making his heart go *thump…thump-thump-thump*.

"Wow. You're not even going to offer me a hand up? If this is what all werewolves are like, I take back what I said about wanting one of my own."

She wanted a werewolf of her own, did she? As a pet—or as a lover? That statement could be taken several different ways, but the scoop neck of her sweater revealing her delicate collarbone had his mind permanently parked on Lover's Lane. As she started to get up, he dragged his mind out of its lust-drunken stupor and took her arm, easing her to her feet. "Sorry about that. You caught me off guard."

"I suppose that's my fault too?" She dusted off her pants and straightened her sweater. "You like to accuse me of things."

"No, that was my fault. I wasn't watching where I was walking, and I'm sorry I bumped into you." Well, he was sorry he knocked her down. Bumping into her had been part of his plan, minus the physical aspect.

"Oh." Her brow lifted. "Well, I'm sorry too." She held his gaze, her soft pink lips moving slightly, trying to form words her mind wouldn't allow her to speak.

"Are you okay?"

"I'm fine." She crossed her arms, jutting her hip to the side, composing herself. "You'll be happy to learn that whatever magical powers I might have, they've never been unbound, so I couldn't possibly have cursed your pack." Her face pinched in an adorable way, and he fought his smile. "Or maybe you won't be happy, since now you have no idea where your friend is. I don't know. I'm not good with people."

She lifted her hands in the air before dropping them at her sides. "It was easier to talk to you when you were a wolf."

"Why do you think that is?" He was fully clothed in jeans and a t-shirt, so she couldn't have been distracted by his body this time. Though he had to admit, she was cute when she was flustered.

She inhaled deeply, letting out a heavy sigh. "It's this witch business. Apparently, I'm supposed to be a fauna witch, but no one ever released my powers. I don't even know why I'm telling you this. It's not like you're deserving of my trust." She bit her bottom lip, searching his eyes.

"Maybe it's because I'm part animal?" It made sense. If her power was with animals, the beast inside him might've been what drew her to him, the reason she'd even speak to him after he accused her of crimes against his pack.

"Maybe. Or maybe it's because my bestie is dead to the world until sundown, and I'm bursting at the seams to talk to her about all this."

"You could talk to me." He opened his arms, trying to

look as inviting as possible. With his height and build, his presence was intimidating to most, but Sophie didn't seem fazed.

"Psh. After you accused me of kidnapping and possible murder? No thanks." Her words said no, but she didn't make a move to leave. In fact, she held his gaze, practically begging him to ply her with questions.

"I'm sorry about that too." He shoved his hands into his pockets. "My pack determined you were to blame, and..."

She crossed her arms. "They sent you to gather evidence."

"I was doing my job, but I didn't find a thing. Jackson is still missing...and this curse..." He shook his head.

"I didn't do it."

"I'm starting to believe you." He reached toward her, touching her arm and stepping to the side, shielding her from the homeless man riding a wobbly bicycle down the sidewalk.

As he whizzed past, her nose scrunched, and she waved a hand in front of her face. "Ugh. Now there's a man who could use a bath. Maybe I should open a bathing business instead. It would help with all the smells out here."

He moved closer to her to replace the aromas of BO and weed with Sophie's delicious scent. The idea of her hands on another man's body didn't sit well with him, and though he knew she was joking, he couldn't ignore the jealousy rolling through his core. *Not good, Trace.* "You being here improves the scent of the French Quarter. Your magic smells amazing. The rest of you does too."

A nervous giggle escaped her throat as she stepped back. "So people tell me. I guess I'm nose blind to it."

"Supes generally can't smell their own magic."

"There is so much I need to learn. So many questions. I can't wait to talk to Jane."

She wasn't the only one with questions. Had her magic been bound so long, she didn't even remember having powers? None of this made sense. He had to keep her talking. "How long has your friend been a vampire? Not long, right?"

"About nine months."

"I've been a werewolf my entire life. I'm sure I can answer your questions."

"I don't know. Jane and I are a team. We do everything together, so I know she can help."

What was this strange dependency on her vampire friend about? Was it because they were both apparently new to the supernatural world, or did it run deeper? And why did he feel the need to explore every nook, cranny, and hidden corner of her mind? "If you're not busy, I'd love to take you to lunch. If your powers really are bound, that's going to change my entire investigation of you."

"I'd think it would end it. No powers, no curse."

If the Alpha called right now and told him Jackson was home and the case was closed, he'd still insist on taking Sophie to lunch. This was a massive red flag flapping in the wind, but he closed his eyes to it, just like he'd closed them to the warning signs with the damn nymph two years ago.

This time was different. He wasn't under a spell, and he could handle himself around Sophie. Hell, he needed to if only to prove to himself he deserved his rank in the pack and a pretty face with a gorgeous body couldn't get in the way of his job. His nostrils flared as he let out a slow breath. After his last conversation with the Alpha, he needed to prove it to her too.

"I'm not ready to end things with you."

"Oh, you're not? Hmm…" Mischief danced in her eyes. "I have exactly ninety-three minutes until I pick up my first client for the afternoon round. That's all I can offer right now."

"I'll take it. We're going to have to head out of the Quarter, though. Can't risk turning into a wolf in the middle of a restaurant, and if you're not the one doing it, I'm still in danger."

"I'm not, so I guess you are. My car is a block away. I'll drive."

Trace gave Sophie directions to Honoré's, his favorite place on Magazine Street. Located in a blue and white, nineteenth-century Victorian mansion, it boasted an expansive front porch dotted with pink and yellow wrought-iron tables and chairs. Inside, his shoes thudded on the original wood floors as they made their way to a corner table in a quiet back room.

Mismatched furniture in shades from dark to light wood to distressed white paint gave the entire restaurant an eclectic vibe, and Trace pulled out a mahogany chair, tucking it under Sophie as she accepted the gesture.

He was doing his job. The Alpha had ordered him to befriend her, so taking her out to lunch was part of the plan. It didn't matter that his pulse sprinted every time he looked into her eyes. So what if her laugh sounded sweeter than jazz music dancing in his ears?

"What?" She smiled, glancing at him over her menu.

"What?" He folded his hands on the table.

"Why are you staring at me like that?"

*Damn it.* He was staring at her, wasn't he? She responded well to flirtation. Might as well keep it up.

"How am I staring?" He arched a brow, and her smile widened, making a fizzy sensation run through his veins.

"If you were in wolf form, I'd assume you wanted a belly rub."

"What if that's exactly what I want?"

She folded her menu on the table, resting her forearms on the surface, mirroring his posture. Leaning forward, she licked her lips and lowered her voice. "Then I hope you'll be in human form and that you'll want more than your belly rubbed."

*Hot damn.* Was it getting warm in here or was this woman on fire? He straightened, dropping his hands in his lap and gripping his thighs to stop himself from reaching for her. Forget lunch. He could make a four-course meal out of Sophie Burroughs. "How much *more* are we talking about?"

Heat sparked in her gaze. "How dirty do you want to be?"

He reached across the table, taking her hand like he'd wanted to a minute ago. "Sex isn't dirty unless you're rolling in the mud."

"Now there's something I haven't tried…yet."

What the ever-loving fuck had he gotten himself into? He was supposed to be questioning her. Sure, she didn't seem to know a thing about his pack's problems, but she could have been an excellent liar. If he admitted Sophie as a lead had gone cold, then he'd have to admit the real reason he was sitting across from her about to share a meal, and he was *so* not ready to go there. *Focus, dickhead. Think with your brain.*

"Tracey, my man." Mike, the restaurant owner and Trace's good friend, sauntered in and shook his hand. His curly, dark brown hair was sheared short on the sides, and his dark eyes sparked red as he swept his gaze over Sophie. "Long time, no see, but I guess this pretty little witch has been keeping you busy. How do you do, ma'am?"

Mike took Sophie's hand, pressing his lips to her skin and inhaling deeply. "She smells divine."

She flashed Trace a quizzical look, and he cleared his throat, hoping to quell the jealousy burning in his chest. Jealousy was not good. Any territorial emotions meant his wolf was jumping on the *let's bang Sophie* train, and if his wolf was on board, they'd be headed for a lot more than banging.

"Mike, this is my friend, Sophie, and we're ready to order." He'd planned on getting his favorite, the fried oyster po-boy, but ingesting a quarter pound of aphrodisiacs when his motor was already humming might lead to disaster. He settled for catfish instead.

Sophie ordered fried shrimp and turned to him as Mike left the room. "Trace is short for Tracey?" Her lips twitched like she was trying not to smile.

He knew exactly where this was going. "It is, and you find it funny. Go ahead and laugh. Get it out of your system."

She let her smile come on full-force, and he forgot to breathe for a moment. "It's weird to see a big, buff guy like you with a girl's name."

He crossed his arms. "It's gender-neutral."

"Is it?" She laughed. "I'm sorry. It shouldn't be funny. See, this is why I'm better with animals."

"Stop apologizing. You're not the first person to make fun of my name, and you won't be the last. Mike called me that on purpose. He's probably right around the corner listening." He raised his voice on the last word, and sure enough, heavy footsteps receded toward the kitchen shortly after.

"Is Mike a werewolf too?"

He narrowed his eyes, studying hers, searching for a hint of dishonesty. She should have smelled the sulfur emanating from his skin like any other supe would. She didn't even flinch when his eyes flashed red, which meant she'd either dealt with plenty of demons or, more likely, she didn't see it happen. "Your powers really are bound, aren't they?"

"Uh, yeah. We've been through this already."

"Mike is a demon."

Her mouth dropped open, her eyes going wide as if this was her first time learning demons existed on Earth. Trace inhaled deeply, searching her scent for signs of deceit, but aside from the remnants of arousal left over from their earlier conversation, she smelled exactly the same.

"You're friends with a demon?" She shook her head. "More importantly, demons are real?"

"Mike's a great guy, as long as you don't make any deals with him. And yes, there are plenty of demons in New Orleans. I'm sure you've met a few."

"If I have, I had no idea. Aren't they…you know… evil? Are we safe eating here?" Her gaze darted about the room like she was on high alert.

"Don't worry. He left hell for a reason, and an angel owns the bakery next door. She keeps him in check."

She sat back in her chair, her voice rising in disbelief. "Get. Out." A woman at a table in the next room leaned over to glare at her, and Sophie covered her mouth, whispering, "Are you serious? Angels and demons walk among us?"

He couldn't fight his smile. She really was clueless

about magic. "Absolutely. They've got some balance between good and evil thing going on that the rest of us try to stay out of."

"Wow. Next you're going to tell me fairies are real too."

"They are."

She giggled. "Unicorns?"

"Only in Montana. They need a lot of room to roam."

"Nymphs?"

He missed a beat in his reply, and his eyes tightened. "They're real too." He straightened, trying to brush off his reaction. Hopefully she didn't notice his change in tone at the mention of the woman who'd nearly cost him his position in the pack. "We're all real, and really good at hiding."

She pursed her lips, eyeing him skeptically. "You have experience with a nymph, don't you?"

*Damn it.* He was not getting into his past mishaps with her. "I've met a few."

She leaned an elbow on the table, resting her chin in her hand. "Tell me about her."

"No." He had defended that woman to the end. Hell, if he'd been under her spell any longer, he might have assisted with her plan to drive the red wolves out of Orleans Parish, and his life would have been over.

His stomach soured as the similarity of his current situation sank in. This time was different though. He felt it. His wolf felt it.

"Okay. We'll put a pin in that one. Maybe I do need my magic unlocked, so I'll be able to tell who's who. Witches have your fancy magic-detecting olfactory sense, right? That's how you can tell?"

He nodded. "And the visible magic in auras, though

that can be hidden. Which is what my pack thought you were doing, since your scent is so strong."

There was no way in hell this sweet, innocent woman had anything to do with the pack curse or his missing friend. Of course, hell also didn't offer him any ways to convince his Alpha of her innocence, and that was a problem. Teresa would send in someone else to do the job if Trace didn't pull through, and he couldn't allow that to happen.

He needed a new plan and fast. "Tell me more about your magic being bound. How did you discover this information?"

She told him a story about being shunned by the witches in the Quarter, finally meeting one willing to talk to her, and learning that witches were born with their powers bound, something he never knew. A real witch would never divulge such sensitive information.

Their food arrived, and between bites, she told him everything she knew about her grandmother, how her best friend came to be a vampire, and her tentative entrance into the supernatural world.

"Is the witch who told you all this in the coven?"

"I think so." She finished the last bite of her shrimp and washed it down with a swig of sweet tea. "She talked like she was."

"It's probably best if you don't tell anyone else about this. You've just let me in on some pretty juicy secrets the coven doesn't want anyone to know." Secrets that could upset the balance of their truce.

"Oops." She covered her mouth with the tips of her fingers.

He flashed her a reassuring smile. "I promise not to tell."

"What about your pack? Don't you have to tell them everything you learned about me, so they'll know I'm innocent?"

He bit the inside of his cheek, his gaze dancing around her face as he tried to formulate a plan. "My pack, and especially my Alpha, are convinced of your guilt. They won't believe me if I tell them otherwise."

"Why won't they believe you?"

"It's a long story."

"It has to do with the nymph, doesn't it?"

He stiffened. For someone who claimed to be bad with people, she could read him like a large print e-book with an audio companion. "How did you know?"

She shrugged. "Your wolf talks to me."

He cocked his head. "Go on."

"I mean, not with words. He just…I don't know. I can sense things from the animal side of you. I know it sounds crazy, but I feel like we have a connection." She dropped her face into her hands for a moment as she shook her head. "Listen to me, I must be crazy thinking I have a connection with a man I've known all of three or four days."

"That doesn't sound crazy at all. I feel it too."

She smiled. "You or your wolf?"

"Both." Though how much of these feelings came from which side, he wasn't yet sure. The man in him found her insanely gorgeous and fun to talk to. His wolf could've felt the connection for one of three reasons. It was either her magic drawing him to her, his mating instincts kicking in, or his magic from the bite running through her veins.

He took her hand across the table and gently ran his finger over the spot where he'd hurt her. "Have you shown any signs that my magic might be taking hold in you?"

"Umm." She tugged from his grasp, folding her hands in her lap and staring at the table.

"You need to tell me if you do, because it's going to throw another wrench into our situation."

She glanced up at him, a questioning look in her gaze.

"My pack doesn't know I bit you, and if they think you cursed us, and you're becoming one of us, they'll want you dead before you shift. I need to know so I can protect you."

"No." She shook her head adamantly. "I'm definitely not sprouting fur or anything like that. This morning, one of my clients started humping my leg, which doesn't usually happen, but other than that, no." She clamped her mouth shut.

"By client, you mean…"

"A dog."

He nodded. "Right. For some reason, I was picturing a man."

She laughed. "That would be something. Oh, now I'm picturing it. Thanks."

"My pleasure." He held her gaze for a moment, and the connection between them seemed to strengthen, tugging him toward her.

Her smile faded. "Your pack wants me dead?"

"My orders were to find Jackson and end your magic by any means necessary, but I believe you, Sophie. After the time we've spent together, after everything you've told me, there's no way you could be involved in this mess."

A look of bewilderment danced in her eyes. "You were planning to kill me?"

"No. Absolutely not." How could he? From the

moment he laid eyes on her at the party, he knew she was special. His wolf wouldn't have let him lay a finger on her in a harmful way.

She leaned away from him, wary. "But the thought crossed your mind."

"I was given an order, but I never intended to obey it. Sophie, if you know anything at all about Jackson or the curse, I need you to tell me. I'm already going to be in deep shit for biting you, and if I go against pack orders and protect you, they might want to take us both out."

"I don't know anything. I swear. If I knew where to find your friend, I would tell you." She paused, chewing her bottom lip and looking thoughtful. "Let me talk to Jane. She runs the club where we first met, so she knows people. She can help."

"I can't get another group of supes involved. This is between the red wolves and the witches."

"She'll be discreet. Trust me, she knows how to handle situations like this, and anyway, *you're* not getting her involved. I am. I have a right to defend myself, so let me help you find Jackson. Then we can prove I had nothing to do with it, and neither one of us will be in trouble."

*Wow.* After everything he'd put her through—sneaking into her house, accusing her, stalking her—she was offering him her help. That said so much about her character. His chest warmed at her generosity, and he couldn't stop the words tumbling from his lips. "Go on a date with me."

She gestured at the table. "I thought that's what this was."

He shook his head. "This was more of an interrogation. Let me take you out on a date. I want to get to know you."

"Aren't you supposed to be hunting for your friend?"

"I am. Every second of my day is spent trying to figure out what happened to him, but I've got to keep up the charade that I'm investigating you."

"Oh." Her posture deflated. "And here I thought you wanted a real date."

*Damn it.* That wasn't how he meant for that to sound. "I do. It'll serve double duty. Let me show you how I would have treated you had we met on better terms." How he could still treat her once this mystery was solved.

She narrowed her eyes, calculating a response. "Saturday night, and in the meantime, I'll help you find your friend any way I can."

"Okay. Saturday night it is. I'm looking forward to it."

She grinned. "Me too."

CHAPTER SIX

Holy chihuahua. What the hell just happened? Sophie's hand trembled as she pulled her phone from her pocket and dialed Jane's number. The call went straight to voicemail, of course, because it was two in the afternoon. "Jane, it's Sophie. I know you're dead right now, but I need you to call me the moment you open your eyes. I've got a problem. A big one." And his name was Trace Thibodeaux.

She shoved the phone into her bag and pulled out her leash as she trotted up the steps to her first client's home. "Hey, Captain." She scratched the shelter dog behind the ears and guided him out the door, a calmness washing over her as the part-lab, part-husky, part-who-knew-what-else nuzzled her hand. "We can figure this out, can't we, boy?"

Captain woofed his agreement, and they walked side by side to the next client's house. She focused, trying to sense the dog's thoughts, to see if she could hear something the way Trace had put his name into her head when he was in wolf form last night. Pausing, she squatted in front of Captain and held his head in her hands, staring into his eyes and willing him to speak in her mind. "Talk to me, boy. I might be one of you by the end of the month."

A slobbery tongue swiping across her cheek was the only response she received. She stood and continued down the sidewalk. Maybe she should have told Trace the truth about the fur that sprouted on her yesterday. Heat flushed her cheeks as she imagined lifting her arms to show him her furry pits. No, she definitely should not have told him. She wasn't even sure if she could trust him yet.

When Sophie had first come to New Orleans, she'd wanted nothing more than to meet all the magical beings who called the Big Easy home. She'd created a fantasy world in her mind, but she'd neglected to consider the dangers that might come with a realm inhabited by creatures with otherworldly powers. That the things going bump in the night weren't always headboards and uglies.

All her life, she'd known she was different. Beyond her affinity for animals and the teasing she'd endured because of it, she'd never felt like she quite fit in anywhere. The fact she never lived in one place more than two years at a time growing up added to it, but deep down, she'd never known anyone she really clicked with besides Jane.

Discovering her grandmother's grimoire gave her hope that she could meet others like herself, and New Orleans was—so she thought—the perfect place to find them. Meeting Crimson, she finally felt like she was on her way in.

Then, she'd met a werewolf like she wanted, one with a seductive grin and hot enough to melt her panties off, and now his pack wanted her dead. Talk about bad luck.

At least she was getting a date out of it. She'd been fully prepared to stay mad at Trace for what he'd done, but all he had to do was look at her with concern in his dark honey eyes, and her will crumbled. He was kind, sweet, funny, and hotter than molten lava. She didn't want *a* werewolf. She wanted Trace.

It was possible—God, how she wanted it to be true—that he was the man from the palm reader's prediction, the one who would make her innermost dreams come true. He obviously fit into her grandmother's prophecy, so why not? Even when she'd consciously tried to be mad at him, their flirtatious banter always drew her in, and she found herself enjoying his company, even when he thought she was a criminal.

Once she talked to Jane, it would all get worked out. They'd find Trace's missing friend and figure out what was going on with the curse. Hell, while they were at it, Crimson would help Sophie unlock her powers, and she'd become a real witch. A member of the coven. She'd find her place in the supernatural world and have a hot werewolf by her side while she did it. Talk about her innermost dream coming true.

She finished her afternoon round and delivered all the clients back to their homes. With thirty minutes to spare before her final round of the day, she plopped onto a bench in Louis Armstrong Park and gazed out over the pond as she rotated her ankles, working the soreness out of her calves. It was time she invested in a new pair of walking shoes.

Her phone buzzed, and she dug it from her bag to find Crimson's name lighting up the screen. She pressed the device to her ear. "Hey Crim, are we still on for tonight? I have a gajillion questions for you."

"I need your help." The sound of drawers opening and closing followed her voice.

"Sure. What do you need?"

"My mom fell and broke her collarbone. I need to fly out to Florida to help my dad with her." More shuffling noises sounded through the receiver.

"Oh, no. Is she going to be okay?"

"Probably, but…can you watch the cat while I'm gone? I hate to put this burden on you, but you're the only one I trust to do it."

"Of course. No problem. Do you want me to stop by and feed him twice a day?"

"Actually, can you take him to your apartment? I don't trust him in my place alone. He's been through a lot."

"Sure. Yeah, I can take him home with me."

"Great. I'm leaving a key under the doormat." A suitcase zipped shut, and footsteps on a wooden floor echoed through the line.

"That's not a safe place to leave a key."

"You're the only one who will be able to find it. I enchanted it."

"Oh, wow." Her shoulders slumped. Just when she thought she was finally going to get some answers, her only hope had to go to Florida. "How long do you think you'll be gone?"

"A few days, tops. And we're still going to talk when I get back, but…this cat is different. He's a familiar, so he's much, *much* smarter than your average feline."

She mentally added getting information about familiars to her laundry list of questions. "Okay. Is there anything else I need to know? Does he have any magical powers of his own? Is that why you don't want to leave him alone?"

"No, he won't cast spells or anything, but don't try to

feed him cat food. He only eats regular people food, so just make a plate for him when you're eating."

"Interesting. Where should I keep his litter box?"

"He uses the toilet."

She laughed. Sure he did. "Does he flush too?"

"Of course. If you turn the water on, he'll wash his paws."

Sophie paused, expecting her friend to laugh, but she sounded as serious as could be. "You're kidding."

"When I get back, we're going to talk, and this will all make sense. I promise."

"I was going to argue that it wouldn't, but with the amount of weird I've seen the past few months, it'll probably make perfect sense. I hope it will, anyway."

"It will. And it's important that the cat stays inside at all times. He can't come into contact with any supes outside your apartment, okay?"

"Got it. I'll keep him indoors and away from people. Anything else?"

"I've been analyzing your magic from the hair you gave me."

Sophie rubbed her head to chase away the phantom stinging sensation. "You mean the hair you yanked from my scalp?"

"If you want to be dramatic, sure."

She laughed. "Drama is my middle name. So, what did you find out? Am I really the chosen one who's supposed to be ruler of all witches?"

"Now, that would be something," Crimson said. "I discovered that your inborn gift is animal communication, like I suspected, so if the cat says anything to you—"

Sophie scoffed. "Animals don't talk to me."

"This isn't an ordinary animal."

"Right. A familiar. You're going to have to explain exactly what that means."

"When I get back. I'm heading out the door now, and I'll call you later to check in. Thank you so much for doing this. I owe you one."

Sophie ended the call and made her way toward her first canine client's home, a little thrill of excitement washing away the disappointment of not getting her questions answered tonight. She was going to cat-sit a witch's familiar, and if that wasn't the coolest thing ever, she didn't know what was.

Not only that, but Crimson said Sophie was the only one she trusted to do it. Surely she had other friends she could have called, but she'd chosen her. Sophie was one step closer to securing a spot in the coven, finding a place where she belonged.

She finished her final round of dog-walking and hurried up the stairs, past her own apartment, to the third floor. Lifting the mat, she found the key where Crimson said it would be. Nothing seemed out of the ordinary. No sparkles exploded from the rug when she moved it. The key didn't glow or feel any temperature other than what a normal key that had been sitting under a doormat for hours would feel. *Bummer.*

With a shrug, she unlocked the door and slipped inside her friend's apartment. Flipping on the lights, she gasped as the overhead lamps illuminated a studio filled with canvases painted in rich hues. Most were landscapes and local landmarks, but a few portraits sat among the array. An easel near the window held an unfinished painting of a man with light brown skin, dark hair, and intense chocolate eyes. He was striking, and the details were so lifelike, it could have been mistaken for a photograph if it were finished.

When Sophie stepped toward the canvas to get a closer look, the cat leapt down from a windowsill, landing in front of the painting and pinning her with an intense yellow-eyed gaze. He meowed, regarding her as if sizing her up, determining whether or not she was a threat.

"Hey, handsome. Remember me? My name's Sophie." She dropped to her knees and held out a hand. "Crimson asked me to look after you while she's away."

The cat slinked toward her, sniffing her hand before darting under the couch.

"Oh, jeez. You probably smell all those dogs, don't you? Let me wash my hands." She glanced at a clock as she stepped into the kitchen. Jane would be waking up soon. With her hands cleaned, she dried them on a dishtowel and returned to the loft area. The cat peered at her from beneath the sofa.

Lying on her stomach, she reached toward him. "You're going to stay with me for a few days. Come on out, little guy."

He swatted a paw at her hand, his claws scraping across her skin.

"Ouch." She jerked her hand away and rose to her feet, flustered. Sure, the cat was a familiar, but he was still an animal, right? "Listen, buddy. You're coming home with me, and we can do it the easy way or the hard way. Don't make me flip this couch over."

Her phone buzzed with a call from Jane. "Hey, girl." Jane yawned. "I haven't even had my morning O neg. What's the problem?"

She reached for the cat again, and it scrambled deeper

beneath the couch. "Ugh, this stupid cat won't come when I call it."

Jane laughed. "A beast you can't tame? Are you sure it's really a cat?"

"It's a familiar. I'm not sure what that means, but it's smarter than a normal cat." She dropped onto the sofa and rubbed her forehead. "Anyway, can you come over? So much happened today, I don't even know where to begin. I saw Trace this afternoon. I think he finally believes I didn't hurt his friend, but now there's a problem with his pack. I just… Can you come over?"

"I'll be there in twenty."

"Thanks, Jane. You're the best." As she pressed end, the cat jumped onto the cushion next to her, cocking its head and looking at her quizzically.

Sophie sighed. "I've got a lot on my plate right now, including a hotter-than-Hades werewolf I can't get off my mind, whose pack might want to kill me for something I'm not even capable of doing. For the love of all that is supernatural in this world, will you please come home with me?"

She held out her arms, and the cat slinked toward her, allowing her to scoop him up and carry him out the door. *Hallelujah.*

She took him to her apartment and set him on the floor. He immediately darted to the kitchen and pawed at the fridge door.

"I'll heat something up for dinner later. Do you want a snack in the meantime?" She opened the refrigerator, and the cat touched the deli drawer with a paw. "All I've got is some ham that's about to expire. Will that work?" She put what was left of the lunchmeat on a paper plate and laid it on the floor.

The cat jumped into a chair, resting his front paws on the table and blinking at her.

"Oh, you like to eat at the table, do you?" She shook her head and put the plate in front of him. "You use the toilet. You eat human food at the table. If you're really a cat shifter, you can turn into a man and stop playing games. I've got enough to deal with right now."

The cat paused from eating, briefly narrowing his eyes at her before returning to the food.

Ten minutes later, Jane arrived, looking fabulous as always. Her vampire complexion, though pale, was as perfect as porcelain, and her shiny brown hair flowed over her shoulders like it belonged on a supermodel.

In the early months after Jane was turned, Sophie had considered asking her friend to bring her into the world of the undead, but drinking blood and sleeping all day wasn't the slightest bit appealing. Plus, the whole being mostly dead thing made their skin clammy like a corpse. She couldn't imagine climbing into bed with a cadaver, much less getting naked with one. She shuddered.

"Are you okay?" Jane touched a frigid hand to her arm, not improving her thoughts.

"I honestly don't know. I—"

The cat crept into the room, freezing as it spotted Jane and arching its back to let out a wicked hiss. Jane smirked, tilting her head in amusement before hissing right back at the cat. With a whiney meow, he jumped onto Sophie's shoulder, digging his claws through her shirt and into her skin as he began a stare down with a vampire.

"It's okay. This is Jane. She's my friend." Sophie pried the cat from her shoulder and set him on the couch. "You're getting good at hissing," she said to Jane. "You sounded just like him."

"Thanks. I've been practicing. It's incredibly satisfying to let one rip when someone's annoying me."

"I can imagine." Sophie turned to the cat and let out a puny human-sounding hiss. He responded by curling into a ball and tucking his paws beneath him.

"Best to leave the hissing to the professionals." Jane sank into a recliner. "So, spill. What's the problem, and how can I help?"

"Remember Crimson, the woman who owns the coffee shop downstairs?"

"The one you think might be a witch? We ought to go up and knock on her door, so I can confirm that theory for you."

"No need. I talked to her about it this morning, and she is a witch." She leaned back on the sofa. "Turns out, I'm one too."

Jane's mouth dropped open. "Seriously? But the spells don't work. What the…? How…?"

"It's a long story, and that's not the biggest issue. The problem is Trace."

"Your sexy werewolf." She wiggled her eyebrows.

Sophie nodded. "I think I've convinced him I'm innocent, but his pack wants me dead." She explained everything she learned today. "So the only way to make them believe I didn't do it is to either find Jackson or find the witch who cursed them. Do you think you can help me?"

The cat crawled into Sophie's lap, placing its front paws on her chest. "Oh, now you want to be my friend? I suppose you feel sorry for me?" She stroked his soft fur, and he purred.

"Wow." Jane crossed her legs, lacing her fingers together on her knee. "The pack doesn't know about your sprouting fur issue? Has that happened again?"

"No, thank goodness. It only happened once. They don't even know Trace bit me. If they knew, I'd be dead by now. He's keeping it a secret to protect me. He's going against pack orders to keep me safe." The cat sat on his haunches, flicking his tail as he watched her intently.

Jane grinned. "Well, isn't that the most romantic thing I've ever heard? You've got the hottest werewolf in New Orleans risking his status in the pack, maybe even risking his life for you. What's his plan if you do turn? Will you run away together? If you do, you can't go too far. I'd miss the hell out of you."

She stared at her hands folded in her lap. "I haven't told Trace about the fur either."

"Why not?"

Heat flushed her cheeks. "It's embarrassing."

"Maybe to you, but I bet it's not to him. His entire body sprouts fur. You having a couple of patches isn't going to faze him."

She lifted her gaze to Jane's. "What am I going to do?"

"You're going to celebrate. I'll work my vampire magic and find the missing werewolf." She held up a hand as Sophie started to protest. "Seriously, don't doubt me. I will be discreet, and I will find out what happened to him. In the meantime, you're going to go on that date, fuck his brains out, and then show him you are everything he's ever wanted in a woman."

She shook her head. "Jane…"

"Think about it. You've met a witch who's willing to help you. You have actual magic inside you that I bet she can help you unlock, and you've caught the eye of one helluva sexy werewolf who's willing to put his life on the line for you. All your dreams are coming true."

"Assuming his pack doesn't kill me."

Jane waved her hand dismissively. "They won't, and if they try, they'll have to get through me, Ethan, and Gaston to get to you. I've got another forty-nine years before I can be on the vampire council, but I've got the Magistrate's ear. Nothing is going to happen to you. You're going to be a badass witch with a werewolf boyfriend by the end of the week."

The cat curled onto her lap, closing his eyes contentedly. Her BFF said exactly the words Sophie wanted to hear, and it was easy to get swept away by her optimism. If everything worked out that way, her dreams would come true, but now that she'd had all evening to think about it…

"I have a feeling it's not going to be that easy."

"You've got this. I know you do." Jane's smile was reassuring, and as her words sank in, Sophie's chest warmed.

There was nothing wrong with optimism. "Thanks, babe. This is why you're my BFF."

"I know. Now, I've got to get out and find dinner before I shrivel up and die again. Are you going to be okay here alone?"

"I'm not alone. I've got Crimson's familiar."

After Jane left, Sophie showered and then found the cat curled up in her bed. There went her idea of breaking out Big Blue while she finished the fantasy she'd just had about Trace. "I guess you won't take up too much room." She picked him up, and, moving him to the side, she climbed under the covers.

Her phone buzzed on the nightstand, and her heart kicked into a sprint when she saw Trace's name lighting up the screen. Clearing her throat, she took a deep breath, trying not to sound too excited. "Hello?"

"Hey, Sophie. I hope it's not too late to call." His deep, velvety voice flowed through her ears like honey.

"It's okay. I was just thinking about you." Dripping wet in the hot shower, he was all she'd thought of.

"You, uh… You were?" Why did the man sound surprised? He was an Earth-bound sex god.

She bit her lip. *Shit.* He apparently didn't call because he was thinking about her. "Yeah. I talked to Jane, and she's going to help find out what happened to your friend."

"Oh." Was that disappointment she detected in his tone? "Great. Are you still willing to help? I thought of something you could do."

"You'd be amazed at all the things I can do." She pressed her lips into a line. Could she not have one conversation with this man without sounding like a nymphomaniac?

His deep chuckle resonated in her soul. "We're still on for Saturday night, right? I'm looking forward to being amazed."

A shiver shimmied up her spine. "Absolutely."

Silence hung between them as she closed her eyes, imagining the fire in his gaze as he trailed his fingers down her cheek, his thumb brushing across her lips before he…

He cleared his throat. "But about finding Jackson. Here's what I need you to do."

CHAPTER SEVEN

Trace stood between two buildings on Burgundy Street, a boutique hotel with a slate gray façade and white wrought iron gallery, and a brown, three-story structure that housed the witch's perfume and secret potion shop on the bottom floor. The gate leading to the alley between stood unlocked, so it was a perfect spot to wait in case the force-shift came on. But every time the goddamn door opened, the overpowering scents of fifty different oils and potions wafted out, singeing his nostrils and making him want to puke.

His heightened canine sense of smell made entering the shop area of the building nearly impossible for a werewolf. The store wasn't enchanted, as far as he knew. The witches relied on the overwhelming aroma to keep other supes from nosing around in their business. Aside from being able to detect magical signatures with their noses, a witch's sense of smell was no better than a human's.

That's where Sophie would come in. It had been years since the red wolves had swiped a copy of the witches' registration manifest, and it was time they updated their records. Sophie would make a perfect distraction while he sneaked in and stole the information.

Truth be told, he'd racked his brain all evening to figure out a way she could help him search for Jackson, not because he actually needed her help, but because he couldn't wait until Saturday to see her again.

He spotted her strutting toward him on the sidewalk, and he tensed, a strange urge to run to her, sweep her into his arms, and carry her away from all this mess making his weight shift to his toes. If his friend hadn't been missing for the past week, he might have done just that.

"Hey." Her smile warmed his soul, and as she stopped two feet in front of him, he fought another urge to lean in and find out if her lips tasted as good as they did in his dreams. She glanced at the perfume shop, her brow furrowing. "I was thinking last night…"

"So was I." He swept his gaze down her body, and a pink flush spread across her cheeks. "You were incredible, too."

She grinned. "It's awfully forward of you to say things like that when we haven't even been on a date yet."

"I can smell your desire, remember?"

He glimpsed a flash of tongue as she moistened her lips, and his knees nearly buckled. She let her gaze meander over him, one brow arching as she seemed to approve of the view. "Can you now?"

"You want me as much as I want you." Okay, maybe he was being too forward, but it was the truth. Every time he flirted with her, her scent warmed like spiced cider. He couldn't help himself.

She laughed and shook her head. "Are you sure you aren't getting my desire mixed up with that awful smell coming from the perfume shop?" She wrinkled her nose.

"Someone must have ordered a horrific combination of scents. I walk by this place every day, and I've never been able to smell it from the sidewalk."

*Interesting.* She shouldn't have been able to smell it at all. His gaze drifted to her arm, where his teeth marks still marred her skin, and hope bloomed in his chest. It shouldn't have. She never asked to be turned into a werewolf, and if she wanted to press charges against him, he'd be so deep in shit, he'd drown. But if she did complete the transformation, and she felt even half of the feelings he felt for her...

"Anyway, I've got another group of dogs to walk in half an hour, so let's get this mission started. All I have to do is distract the women behind the counter?"

"Right. I'll slip in the back and find the manifest, photograph it, and then I'll text you when I'm out."

She crossed her arms. "How do you know it's even in there? Wouldn't they keep something like that in their coven headquarters? Or, more likely, on a computer?"

"You'd be surprised how backward supes can be, and they don't keep it at the coven house because that would be the first place people would look for it." He stepped toward her, resting his hand on the small of her back, his touch making her scent flare again. *Delicious.* "Being a cop in the NOPD pays the bills, but I'm also the head of security for the pack. If a supe orgasms within a ten-mile radius of New Orleans, my men know."

She pressed her lips together, suppressing a smile. "I love it when you talk dirty. Tell me more."

A shudder ran through his body, and he dropped his arm. As much as he enjoyed the flirtatious banter with this incredible woman, they had a job to do. "The manifest contains the names of every registered witch in Orleans

Parish. When my men sniffed you out, the coven already knew about you. They said you were unregistered and that you were a dud. We assumed you were the only one, but now I'm thinking there may be more people like you. People who possess magic but don't know it or can't access it."

"I know I have magic." She lifted her chin.

"But you didn't until yesterday. If magic has to be unlocked, there's a chance someone on that list figured out how to unbind her powers, under the coven's radar, and she's the one responsible for the curse on my pack."

"How do you even know I'm on the list? There could be dozens of people like me roaming the city. The only difference with me is that I went looking for it."

He shook his head. "We aren't the only ones with informants. Supes of every variety work for a common goal: to identify everyone in the city who possesses magic. I promise you the first day you were here, probably within the first few hours, you'd been identified and added to the manifest. Your scent but lack of signature in your aura suggested you were trying to hide your magic, but the witches must have known your powers were bound... something the werewolves never would have figured out."

"So if I could unbind my powers and hide my aura, the coven would never know I had magic?"

"And you'd be a threat to us all. Our truces keep everything in balance, which is why the curse on my pack could be detrimental to the entire city."

"Isn't sneaking in and photographing their private documents against the truce?"

He grinned. "Only if we get caught."

Holy fur and fangs, Sophie was working with a supe, doing sneaky supe things, dangerous things. What would happen to them if they got caught? Would the war start between the werewolves and the witches? If it did, which side would she be on?

She sucked in a deep breath and blew it out hard. These were questions she should have thought to ask before Trace bounded down the alley toward the back entrance, but her rational mind went into hiding every time she was near the man.

*Suck it up, buttercup. You're in this now.* She'd offered to help, and he was depending on her. Maybe he'd reward her later…

*Focus, Soph.* She gripped the cool metal door handle and tugged it open, pausing as a blast of fragrances assaulted her senses like a forcefield over the entrance. How did these women work in here all day?

She swallowed the sour sensation creeping up her throat and forced her way through the stench and into the shop. Two witches stood behind the counter, a petite one with dark eyes and jet-black hair styled in an asymmetrical pixie cut, and one about the same height as Sophie, with striking blue eyes and long brown hair. Of course, the only reason Sophie knew they were witches was because Trace told her they were, but they must have sensed her witchy scent.

Both their heads snapped up at the same time, and the brunette narrowed her eyes at Sophie briefly before plastering on a smile. "Hey there. How can we help you?"

"Umm." Sophie glanced around at the shop. Rows of wooden shelves containing small glass bottles with cork stoppers covered two of the walls, and an archway the width of two normal doors led into a back room. Trace peeked from behind the wall and gave her a thumbs-up before disappearing again.

She cleared her throat and faced the witches. "I'm looking for a special perfume to make a man want me."

"Oh, honey, you've come to the right place." The pixie cut sashayed around the counter and offered Sophie a postcard and pen. "I'm Jade, and this is Audrey. Why don't you fill out this card so we can mix something up for you?"

"Sure." Sophie took the pen and wrote her real name on the top of the page. As she got to the "S" in "Burroughs," she froze, pressing the tip into the paper harder and harder until blue ink pooled around it. What kind of supernatural spy gave the enemy her real name?

*Shit.* She tightened her grip on the pen, finishing the S and forcing herself to breathe. It wasn't like she could scratch it out and write Pussy Galore instead.

"Is everything okay?" Jade linked her fingers, staring at Sophie intently.

"Yeah. Just a little headache." She finished the form with a fake address and phone number. "I don't know how you ladies make it through the day with all these wonderful scents."

"You get used to it." Jade took the card and strode toward the archway. Toward Trace.

*Crap.* "Why are you taking that to the back room?" She nearly shouted to warn him. Hopefully the witches didn't notice the panic in her voice.

Jade paused, turning to face her. "I'm just going to enter this in our customer database. Audrey will take care of you."

Sophie glimpsed Trace darting from one side of the

arch to the other. Damn, he was fast. Not as fast as a vampire, but the man could move.

"Tell me a little about your tastes, Sophie." Audrey smiled, her gaze flicking to Jade before she focused on Sophie again. "Do you like floral scents or something warmer?"

Sophie glanced to the backroom as Jade pulled out an ancient-looking binder and flipped through the pages, running her finger from top to bottom as if reading a list. It must have been the manifest Trace was looking for. "Floral. No, I think the man I'm after prefers warmer scents."

Audrey nodded. "If men only knew what we go through to impress them."

"She's fine." Jade strutted into the shop area, mouthing something to the other witch that Sophie couldn't decipher.

If Sophie was going to be a spy, she'd need to work on her lipreading skills. Judging by the softening of both their demeanors, Jade had found Sophie's name already on the list, and they knew she was harmless. Correction: they *thought* she was harmless. She stifled a giggle. This spy stuff was fun.

"Let's mix you up something magical," Jade said. "What's this guy like?"

Sophie turned, angling herself so she faced the archway straight on and forcing Jade and Audrey to put their backs toward Trace, who pulled out his phone to snap pictures of the manifest Jade had left on the desk. These witches were so confident, they were careless.

"Oh, he's tall and built, with auburn hair and a full beard. The man oozes masculinity. He's a cop too. Sexy as hell. My panties want to drop to the floor on their own every time I'm near him, if you know what I mean." She grinned as Trace stifled his chuckle, and she forced herself to hold eye contact with the women.

"Sounds scrumptious," Jade said.

"You have no idea."

"You said you wanted something to make the man want you." Audrey ran her fingers along a row of bottles, stopping on a brown one with a white label. "What kind of *want* are we talking about? Is this purely sexual, or are you looking for more?"

Trace stopped, standing in the door with a brow arched as if he were seriously interested in the answer to her question.

Sophie locked eyes with him for half a second before casting her gaze to the row of bottles, lest she give him away. "I'm not sure how he feels, but I think I want more. I mean, the initial attraction was pure lust, but now that I'm getting to know him…"

Audrey's smile urged her to continue, though she didn't dare look to see if Trace still stood exposed. "I feel a connection with him. Like maybe he could be…" She almost said *the one*, but she bit her tongue to stop the words from escaping. That would be a sure-fire way to send him running with his tail between his legs. "He could be someone I'd like to date more than once, you know?"

"Girl, I know." Audrey took another bottle from the shelf as Sophie's phone buzzed in her pocket.

She checked the screen and found a text from Trace: *All done, gorgeous. You were amazing.* Her stomach fluttered.

"Oh, crap. I have to go." She shoved the phone into her pocket. "Just, umm…hold off on the perfume. I'll be back. Maybe." She scurried out the door, adrenaline making it feel as though her feet didn't touch the floor.

Glancing at her watch, she cursed under her breath and powerwalked toward her first client's home. She had three minutes to pick the dog up if she was going to be on time for this walk.

Her phone buzzed again with a text from Trace: *Where did you go?*

She replied: *I have to work. Talk later.*

Her heart beating like a racehorse's hooves, she made it to her destination right on time. Her excited energy rubbed off on the dogs, and she nearly had to jog to keep up with them as they made their afternoon round. Even with the extra boost of adrenaline, the male dogs kept their private parts to themselves, and Sophie's legs remained safe from their wanton advances.

Her smile didn't fade all day. The entire mission—how exciting was it to call what they'd done a mission?—had lasted no more than twenty minutes, but Sophie couldn't remember the last time she'd had that much fun. Catching glimpses of Trace as he gathered evidence for his pack had been a major turn-on too. The man was lucky she had to work, or she might have torn his clothes off right there on the sidewalk when it was done.

Then again, depending on how much of her conversation with the witches he heard, maybe *she* was the lucky one. What if Saturday night's date was nothing more than his attempt to get into her pants? Or worse, what if everything...the flirting, the heated gazes...what if it was all part of his spy persona, and he still thought she was to blame? What if the Trace she was starting to fall for wasn't the real Trace at all?

*Oh, get over yourself.* He'd already scoured her apartment and found nothing. At the very least, she could get a good lay out of the situation, and at best… Who knew? She might as well enjoy the rush while it lasted.

She finished her evening round and picked up some Chinese takeout with an extra serving of chicken fried rice for the cat. He meowed his appreciation and ate at the table next to her—*so weird*—before she took a quick shower and collapsed into bed. The cat crawled onto her stomach, curling up and rubbing the top of its head against the bottom of her boob.

She laughed and stroked its fur. "That's the most action I've gotten in months, but things might be changing soon. If Crimson isn't back by Saturday night, you'll need to make yourself scarce. Understand?"

The cat blinked at her, and her phone rang from the nightstand, Trace's name lighting up the screen. She pushed the cat aside to answer. "Hey there, hot stuff."

"Hello, beautiful. How was your day?" How could his voice be deep and rumbly, yet smooth as satin at the same time?

"Adventurous, actually. I had my first foray into the supernatural spy world, and it was quite thrilling."

He chuckled. "You were amazing in there. I could use you on my team."

Her lips parted on a quick inhale, excitement buzzing through her veins. "Really?"

"Yeah. If you become a werewolf, I'll hire you at the next full moon."

"Oh." Her chest deflated with her sigh. "I don't think that's going to happen." Nor did she want it to. Becoming a full-fledged witch was her number one priority. She could imagine the looks on Jade's and Audrey's faces when she strolled into the perfume shop, magic sparkling in her aura. *See if they underestimate me again.*

"Well, either way, I appreciate your help. I found three new names added to the roster since we last swiped a copy: you plus two others. I checked out one of them this afternoon, but I didn't find a trace of Jackson. I plan to drop in on the other one tomorrow."

Her chest tightened as she pictured the way he'd *dropped in* on her. Was that jealousy stirring in her belly? Surely not. "I hope you're not crawling into their beds naked like you did mine." Her teeth clicked as she clamped her mouth shut. They weren't a couple. It was none of her business how he conducted his.

A deep belly laugh resonated through the receiver. "Would it bother you if I did?"

"Yes, as a matter of fact, it would. You're starting to grow on me, wolfman."

He inhaled deeply, the sound tickling her ear. "I grow every time I'm near you, *cher*."

She couldn't help but giggle. "Do you now?"

"Yes, ma'am. You tend to have that effect on me."

"I'd like to see for myself." She fisted her hand and bit her finger to contain her excitement.

"I can show you Saturday night."

"Is that a promise?" She dropped her head back on the pillow, grinning at the ceiling.

"It most certainly is."

CHAPTER EIGHT

Trace jogged up the steps to Sophie's apartment and blew against his palm, attempting to check his breath for the third time since he'd gotten out of his truck. Like the first two times, he couldn't smell a damn thing, but he popped a mint into his mouth just in case.

He'd been a bundle of nerves all day, the anticipation of seeing Sophie in a nonwork, non-accusing capacity winding him up tighter than a gator's ass in a hurricane. Inhaling deeply, he straightened his spine, composing himself. He was the Alpha's right-hand man and First Lieutenant in his pack. He didn't show his nerves to anyone, especially not the woman he was trying to claim…err…seduce. The woman he was trying to *seduce*.

He shook his head and lifted a hand to knock, but before his knuckles met wood, the door swung open. Sophie beamed a smile, and his gaze swept the length of her feminine form, taking in the short red dress and matching heels that made her legs look ten miles long. She rested her hand against the door jamb, and he glimpsed polished red nails that matched her outfit perfectly.

Her long blonde hair was swept up in a twist with a few soft strands framing her face, and she held a tiny gold purse attached to her wrist by a thin strap.

She was stunning. Beautiful. Magnificent. The most gorgeous woman he'd ever seen, but the signal from his brain to his mouth was fried, and the only word he managed to utter was, "Damn."

"That is exactly the response I was hoping for. Who needs designer perfume?"

"Definitely not you."

She peered over her shoulder and pulled the door shut, joining him on the landing. "I guess we better get you out of the French Quarter in case the evil witch works her magic again."

"Hold on. I need to do something first." Something he'd been wanting to do since the moment he met her. An urge he'd been struggling with for as long as he'd known her, and damn it, he was tired of fighting.

Cupping her cheek in his hand, he leaned in and pressed his mouth to hers. He only meant for it to be a quick brush of the lips, but when "*mmm*" vibrated from her throat and she threw her arms around his neck, he went for it, tongue and all.

She leaned into him, pressing her soft curves into his chest, parting her lips and drinking him in like she was dying of thirst. He didn't realize how parched he'd been until her velvet tongue brushed against his, sending a tidal wave of emotion rolling through his body. It crashed into his core, and his inner wolf howled in delight.

"You're not wasting any time, are you?" She rested her forehead against his.

"I couldn't help myself. You look good enough to eat."

She laughed and pulled away, smoothing her dress

down her stomach. "While I'm tempted to drag you inside right now and let you make a meal out of me, I'm starving. I want dinner before I put out."

"I like a woman who knows what she wants."

Resting a hand on her hip, she trailed her gaze down his form, lingering below his belt. "I know exactly what I want."

"I can't wait to give it to you."

"Dinner first." Rising onto her toes, she swiveled around and strutted toward the staircase, the quick movement wafting her delicious cinnamon fragrance to his senses.

Oh, he'd take her to dinner. Then *she* would be dessert. "Hold on."

She spun to face him. "Yes?"

He focused on the sexy red high heels, silently cursing himself for what he was about to suggest. "I was thinking we'd go for a stroll in City Park after dinner. As much as I love those shoes on you…"

She looked down at her feet, twisting one inward in a way that made his mouth water. "Good call. Stilettoes aren't made for long walks. Give me a sec." She strutted inside her apartment and returned two minutes later in a pair of silver ballet flats. "Thanks for the warning. You'd have ended up carrying me if I'd tried to wear those heels all night."

"If you want to put them back on later, I won't mind."

She laughed. "I bet."

He took her to Marie's, a small mom and pop Creole joint a few miles north of the Quarter. Quiet and unassuming, Marie's had the best crawfish bisque and court bouillon in town. Sophie asked him questions about his life, and she did a damn good job feigning interest as he droned on about pack life and his boring upbringing. He grew up in one house near the river, and he barely moved two miles away from his parents when he left the nest, which was typical for red wolves. They stuck together.

Sophie told him fascinating stories about traveling the world when her dad was in the military, experiencing a new place every couple of years. Trace didn't even have a passport.

She finished the last bite of her shrimp Creole and traced her finger around the rim of her wine glass. "I can't even imagine what a life like yours would be like."

He chuckled. "Boring. Routine."

She tilted her head. "With stability. Always knowing where you belong. Fitting in. I never had that growing up. I still feel like I don't."

"Why do you think that is?"

"I'm a witch with no powers who's better at talking to animals than people, for one thing."

"You're great with people." He reached for her hand across the table. "You've got me hooked."

"We'll see how long you stick around."

*Forever.* He clenched his teeth. The word had nearly slipped from his lips, and that would have been the end of his blossoming relationship with Sophie right then and there. He had to play it cool, but he needed her to know he was after more than her body.

Lacing his fingers through hers, he looked into her eyes. "I'm not going anywhere any time soon."

She held his gaze for what felt like an eternity before a sly smile curved her lips and she winked. "Great. I've landed myself a clingy one."

"Just call me Saran Wrap." He laughed, and she

laughed, the tension between them dissolving like sugar in hot coffee. "You can't be that bad with people."

"Don't underestimate me."

"What's the most embarrassing thing you've done lately?"

She straightened her spine, smoothing her napkin in her lap as her eyes tightened. "The night Jane met Ethan, I puked on his shoes."

Trace blinked, trying to keep a neutral expression, but damn… "Okay, that is bad. What happened?"

"It was our first night in New Orleans, and it was Mardi Gras." She shrugged, and an adorable blush tinted her cheeks.

He nodded. "Gotcha. No need to say more. We've all been there."

"What about you?"

"Oh, I'm pretty calm and collected. You have to be in my line of work."

"Uh-uh. I'm not buying it for a minute, and you're not getting out of this." She crossed her arms. "I shared. Now it's your turn."

He couldn't have told her no if he tried. The problem was, aside from the incident with the nymph, which he wasn't about to bring up, he hadn't done much to screw up. Cupping his chin in his hand, he rubbed his beard and searched his memory for something embarrassing. "I found myself naked in the bed of the most beautiful woman I've ever met, and instead of asking her to join me, I accused her of crimes against my pack. I'm still working on earning her forgiveness."

"Wow. Sucks to be her. I can't imagine what I'd do if a hot, naked werewolf wound up in my bed. If he accused me of crimes against his pack, I might threaten to beat him with a vibrator." She grinned. "I forgive you."

He chuckled. "Good."

"Still no luck finding your friend?"

"I feel like I'm chasing my tail. Every time I get a lead, it comes up dry, and I keep running in circles."

"Did you ever stop to think that maybe he doesn't want to be found? That maybe he and the witch ran away together, and they're sipping margaritas on a beach in Mexico?"

He looked at the woman sitting across from him, with her sky-blue eyes and electric smile. He'd had the same thoughts about her recently, whisking her away from danger, taking her somewhere no one could hurt her, especially his pack. If it came down to it, and Sophie were in real danger, he'd do just that. "I suppose it's a possibility, though I like to think he'd at least let me know he was okay."

And it still didn't answer the riddle of why someone was force-shifting the members of his pack. He glanced at a clock. "Oh, we've got to get going, or we'll miss our appointment."

"Our appointment for what?"

"You'll see." He stood, taking her hand again and tugging her to her feet. He'd mull over the idea that his best friend might have ditched him on purpose later. Right now, his focus was on his own beautiful witch.

They made the short drive to City Park and strolled up the trail toward Big Lake, where the gondola he'd booked for the hour awaited them. When he stepped up to the ticket booth and gave the attendant his name, a brown tabby jumped onto the counter, arching his back and hissing.

"Sylvester, what's wrong with you?" The attendant scooped up the cat, dropping him on the floor, and passed Trace a waiver to sign. "I'm sorry. He's a friendly cat. I don't know what's gotten into him." A deep mewling sound emanated from the cat's throat as it glared at Trace.

"It's okay. I'm not really a cat person." He signed the form and took the tickets from the attendant.

"You don't like cats, or they don't like you?" Sophie slipped her hand into his as they walked out on the pier toward the gondola.

"Both. Werewolves and cat shifters are natural-born enemies. We've never gotten along as far as I know."

Her eyes widened. "That was a shifter?"

He laughed. "That was a domesticated house cat, but animals can sense the wolf in me. Of course, we werewolves think we're better than cats. I'm sure the cats feel superior to us too."

"Cats feel superior to everyone." She stopped, slipping from his grasp, her brow furrowing. "I'm cat-sitting for my neighbor. He's a familiar. Is that going to be a problem later?"

"A familiar? I thought you weren't friends with any witches?" He gestured toward the boat, where a short man in a black and white striped shirt waited with his arm outstretched.

"Just the one who told me the secrets I spilled to you." Sophie took the man's hand and stepped into the gondola. "She lives upstairs, but she texted me earlier. She'll be home tomorrow morning."

"I don't have much experience with familiars, but a cat's a cat." He joined her in the boat, sinking into the seat and wrapping an arm around her shoulders.

"I'd say maybe we should go to your place after this,

but I don't want to leave him alone all night. If he gives us any trouble, I'll put him in the bathroom."

"That's a good place for a feline."

The gondolier played soft Italian music on a speaker as he paddled the boat around the lake, and Sophie leaned into Trace's side, a contented sigh escaping her lips as she rested a hand on his thigh.

A walking trail surrounded the water, dotted with massive oaks to provide plenty of shade in the daytime, and the New Orleans Museum of Art stood in the distance, it's white stucco façade and Grecian columns illuminated against the darkness.

Everything about this felt right. The clear night sky twinkled with stars, and the moon, three-quarters full, shone bright, casting a silvery glow on the lake. Sophie fit next to him like she was made to be there, and for a moment, despite the turmoil in his pack, all felt right in the world.

"Why did you decide to become a cop?" She angled her face toward him and crossed her legs, hooking her ankle over his.

His chest tightened at the intimate gesture. "It's in my blood. My dad's a cop too, and it helps the pack, and all supes, to have people on the inside."

Her gaze flicked back to the gondolier, and she tensed.

"He's a water sprite," he whispered.

She turned to look at him, narrowing her gaze as if trying to see his magic. He waved, and she waved back before settling into Trace's side again. "Do any of the human police know what you are?"

"Just the chief, and he's sworn to secrecy like the mayor and the governor."

"Jane's dad is the governor of Texas. Imagine how

shocked she was to learn that he knew about y'all all along and never told her." She laughed. "She was pissed."

"I can imagine. What about you? I'm surprised with your animal abilities, you didn't become a vet."

She let out a slow breath. "My animal abilities caused me so much trouble when I was young, I wanted nothing to do with them. Walking to school, stray dogs would follow me. We had a swarm of cats hanging around outside our house no matter where we lived, and I got teased because of it. I got called 'Dog Girl,' 'Crazy Cat Girl,' 'Dr. Dolittle Junior.'"

"Jeez. Such original names."

"I know, right? By the time I got into high school, I didn't have any friends. When I would start getting close to someone, it never failed. We either moved away, or I'd forget most people don't talk to animals as if they actually understand them, and they'd decide I was a weirdo. Then came Jane." A wistful look crossed her face.

"You two seem really close."

"She saved me. She took me in, and she wasn't the slightest bit put off by my quirks. At school, she was the epitome of popularity: rich, her dad was in politics, she had four hot older brothers. Everyone wanted to be her friend, but she dealt with a lot of fake people. She liked me because I was real. Her mom died when she was young, and she came to my house a lot. My mom was a mother figure for her, and we were like sisters." She looked at him, and he nodded, silently urging her to continue.

"Anyway, we were roommates in college, and I majored in business. I walked dogs on the side to earn money—I wasn't born into wealth like Jane—and the business did so well, I couldn't see myself working in a cubicle in an entry-level job when I was making a good living already. So I focused on the business and expanded, and now I'm working on a branch here in New Orleans."

"What made you decide to branch out here?"

"I moved here to be with Jane. Well, that and…" She shrugged.

"And what?" His curiosity piqued, he angled his body toward her to see her face.

"It's silly." She cast her gaze downward and drew circles on his thigh with her finger. "I saw a fortune teller in Austin. She told me my business would prosper here, and I'd find magic and a man to make my innermost dreams come true. God, saying it out loud makes it sound crazy."

"That's not silly at all. Or crazy. I've met plenty of fortune tellers who know what they're talking about." He tugged her closer and kissed the top of her head. "Was she right?"

She shrugged. "Business is starting to pick up. I've discovered plenty of magic."

"And the man?"

She lifted her head from his shoulder and searched his eyes. "I'll let you know."

He could be that man. He *wanted* to be that man.

As the boat ride ended, he tipped the sprite and tucked Sophie under his arm, guiding her down a path into the deeply wooded area of the park. Massive oak trees, some as old as eight hundred years, towered above them, their canopies reaching out to touch the branches of their neighbors, creating a natural archway along the gravel path. Spanish moss draped from the boughs like curtains, and tiny new oaks sprouted around the roots.

The sharp scent of ginger and vinegar reached his senses, and he froze, tightening his grip on Sophie. He'd recognize the smell of that magic anywhere, and date or not, it was his job to deal with it. Something rustled in the bushes to the right, and he tugged Sophie off the path, undoing the first two buttons of his shirt before slipping it over his head and handing it to her.

Sophie gave him a quizzical look. "I fully intended on putting out tonight, Trace, but here in the park? Aren't you even going to kiss me first?"

"Wait here." He kicked off his shoes and jogged into the brush before shifting into his wolf form and shimmying out of the rest of his clothes.

CHAPTER NINE

Wait here? Did he seriously just tell her to *wait here*? Who did this guy think he was? She did not spend the past two and a half hours pouring her heart out to him, letting herself fall for the guy, only for him to turn into some testosterone-laden alphahole who thought women were helpless little creatures who needed to be protected and should *wait here*. If danger lurked in them there woods, she wasn't about to let him face it alone.

Clutching his shirt in her hand, she took a moment to press it to her nose and bask in his delicious scent. Hey, he was the hottest guy in New Orleans. She couldn't help herself. Warm and woodsy, with a hint of pine, it was a smell that made her insides melt every time she got near him. *Yum.*

With the obligatory shirt sniff out of the way, she fisted it in her hand—because she was supposed to be mad at him for his caveman act—and marched into the woods where Trace had disappeared.

Branches scratched at her bare legs, and her feet sank into the soft soil as if she were walking on a sponge. Thank goodness she'd changed into flats, though even they would probably be ruined after this trek through the brush.

She stopped at the edge of a clearing and found Trace in his wolf form, a ridge of copper fur standing on end along his back. He bared his teeth in a snarl, and Sophie wondered how she'd thought him a domesticated animal at all before. He looked absolutely wild.

Standing across from him, with its back arched and a paw with razor-sharp claws lifted—in defense or offense, she couldn't tell—was the biggest brown kitty she'd ever seen. Denser than a house cat, it had muscular shoulders and thick legs, and a ring of fur accented its face, like a smaller version of a lion's mane. This mini lion sported spots like a jaguar, but it couldn't have weighed more than twenty pounds. Compared to Trace's sixty or seventy pounds of pure canine muscle, the fight hardly seemed fair.

"Is that a bobcat?" They were the only kind of wild cats she knew of in Louisiana. It was way too small to be a cougar. "Are you a shifter or a regular cat?"

She didn't expect an answer from either of them, but Trace's voice faintly echoed in her head. *She's a bobcat shifter, and she's in our territory looking for a fight. I've dealt with her and her sisters before. Give me five minutes.*

"She?" Sophie crossed her arms, a stab of jealousy slicing through her chest. She had no right or reason to be jealous, but there the emotion was, clawing its way into her heart. Exactly how had he *dealt* with her before? Damn it, she liked this guy way too much.

The cat woman hissed and swatted her paw at Trace, who growled in return.

"Oh, no. This is not happening." Sophie moved closer to them and shook a finger at the cat. "First of all, both of you are really messing with my fantasy that shifters turn into ginormous beasts that can rip your head off with a snap of their jaws. I feel like a giant watching the two of you."

Trace's lip curled as he gave her the side-eye, and the cat woman mewled deep in her throat.

"And second, how the hell did you just put thoughts in my mind? I *heard* you, Trace." She'd heard the actual words as he spoke them. When he told her his name before, it had felt like the thought came from her own mind.

*"It's part of your magic."* She clutched her head as he spoke again.

"Okay, that's something we're going to have to discuss later, because wow. That's cool." She focused on the cat. "Listen. I'm on a date with this man, and I do not want him getting into a fight when he's supposed to be getting into my pants. Whatever beef you have with him and his pack, you need to get over it and move along. This isn't happening right now." She wagged her finger between the two of them to indicate the possible fight she was trying to defuse.

"Both of you need to chill out. Take a deep breath with me." She inhaled, and a slight vinegary scent mixed with the woody outdoor smells. Whether or not Trace and the cat lady followed along, she couldn't tell, but the cat's back began to de-arch, and Trace's ridge of upright fur smoothed.

"Okay. Now we're getting somewhere. I understand this is a territory dispute, so I want you to leave, ma'am. If you have issues with the truce or pact or whatever it is you have with the wolves, you can take it up with the Alpha in a civilized manner. Now go. Scoot." She waved an arm at the cat woman, who turned and bounded away.

Trace sat on his haunches and cocked his head at Sophie.

"You need to turn back into a human and get dressed before someone sees you. If you're coming back to my place, I want you as a man this time." She spun around and stomped toward his discarded clothes. "And don't you ever tell me to *wait here* again, mister. Just because I'm a woman, it doesn't mean I'm defenseless."

"It has nothing to do with you being a woman."

Sophie bent down to pick up Trace's pants. When she turned around, she found him in human form—naked human form—looking at her with an expression of awe. Of course, her gaze didn't linger on his face long. The moonlight filtering through the trees illuminated his figure, giving him an ethereal glow. All that muscle. The trail of auburn hair leading down to his...

Yep. He was hung like a horse, just as she remembered. She swallowed hard.

"Can I have my clothes, please?"

When she didn't respond, a cocky smile tilted his mouth as he took the fabric from her hands. "I assume I should take you being speechless as a compliment?"

She blinked, watching his muscles bunch and extend as he dressed. "You're hot, Trace, and I think you know it."

He chuckled. "Still like hearing it, especially from you."

"What was that about? Was the cat woman your ex-girlfriend or something? Is that why you didn't want me to follow you?"

A disgusted look contorted his features. "Cats and wolves are *not* compatible in any way. Especially in the bedroom. I didn't want you to follow me because I've dealt with her before. I was afraid if she sensed my feelings for you, she'd attack you to hurt me."

"Why would attacking me hurt you?"

He looked at her as if she'd gone insane. "Because I care about you."

"Oh." She clamped her mouth shut. Reciprocation would have been the nice thing to do. She did care for the man, after all. But his sudden confession took her aback, and her brain and her mouth seemed to be operating on different channels.

He buttoned his shirt and rolled the sleeves up to his elbows. "How did you calm us down like that?"

"What do you mean?"

"My wolf was ready to attack, and I know she was too. Then you came along and told us to calm down, and my wolf obeyed. Even the cat listened. Cats never listen."

"I don't know, I just talked to y'all. I guess because you were in your animal form, I was more persuasive." She shrugged.

"You're amazing. Have I told you that yet?"

Her stomach fluttered. He cared about her, and he thought she was amazing. It seemed she wasn't the only one interested in more than sex from this pairing. "I don't think you have." She grinned and batted her lashes.

"You're incredible." Grasping her hips, he tugged her to his body and wrapped his arms around her waist. "Magnificent."

"Tell me more."

"How about I show you?" He brushed his lips to hers, the coarse hairs of his beard tickling her skin as he coaxed her mouth open with his tongue. He tasted like a peppermint breath mint, and the warmth of his strong arms enveloping her was enough to make her knees buckle.

She leaned into him, running her hands across his strong back and down his muscular arms. The man was hard all over, especially the steel rod pressing into her hip, making her think naughty thoughts. She'd seen this man naked twice now, and she'd yet to touch him. It was time that changed.

Pulling away, she sucked her swollen bottom lip into her mouth, and he gazed at her with hooded eyes, a passion-drunk smile crooking his mouth. "Take me home." She nipped his earlobe before slipping her hand into his.

"That's an excellent idea." His voice was husky. "We've probably had enough excitement for the night."

"Oh, honey. The excitement hasn't even begun." She grinned and strolled to the path leading to the parking lot, tugging Trace along behind her. "Why are you hesitating?"

He gazed at her ass. "The view is nice from back here."

She laughed. "It's even better from the front. I'll show you when we get home."

"I'm not sure I'll make it that long."

They climbed into Trace's truck, and he texted his Alpha to warn her about the intruding bobcat shifter before driving back to Sophie's apartment. As she opened the front door, she glimpsed the backside of Crimson's cat as he dove under the couch, out of sight. Hopefully he'd stay there.

Trace paused in the entry, lifting his nose as if sniffing the air. "I smell magic."

"Crimson's familiar is here. Maybe that's what you smell?" She closed the door and tugged him into the living room.

"Maybe. It's muddled. I've never smelled anything quite like it." He stepped past the couch the cat hid beneath and stroked the backs of his fingers down Sophie's cheek. "What do you want to do now?"

A shiver ran down her spine, making heat bloom below her navel. She'd wanted this man from the moment they met. There was no sense in playing hard to get now. "You, Trace. I want to do you in every way imaginable… and believe me, I've imagined plenty."

"Have you?" Mischief sparkled in his eyes as he moved toward her, pinning her to the wall with a hand on either side of her head. "With your legs wrapped around my waist, using the wall for leverage?" He swept his gaze down her body before returning to her eyes.

Jesus Christ, the man hadn't laid a finger on her, and her panties were already wet. "That's one way to do it." She touched his face, gliding her fingers across his forehead and cupping his cheek in her hand.

He closed his eyes, nuzzling into her palm as if he relished the affection. "Bent over the couch with me taking you from behind?"

"Mm-hmm." She undid the buttons on his shirt, running her hands across his pecs and down his abs. He inhaled deeply, his lids falling shut again as she explored his body. "And over the table. The bathroom counter was fun too, with the mirror and all."

"You have a vivid imagination." He shrugged off his shirt, dropping it on the floor.

She ran a finger along the waistband of his jeans, and his stomach tightened with her touch. "I'm a daydreamer."

He closed the distance between them, gliding his lips along her neck before tugging down the zipper on the back of her dress. "Let me make your dreams come true."

*Oh, hell yes.* She shimmied out of her dress, letting it pool around her feet, and Trace stepped back, drinking her in with his gaze.

An appreciative grunt sounded in his chest as he shook his head slowly, and a crooked smile tilted his lips. "My imagination's got nothing on reality. You are even more gorgeous than I envisioned."

Her cheeks warmed at his words. She'd had her share of casual sex and heard plenty of shallow compliments aimed at getting between her legs, but something about the way Trace said it, the way he looked at her, she believed he meant every word.

"Well, let's finish unwrapping, and I'll gift you with the best sex of your life." She popped open her bra and tossed it aside.

Trace's pupils dilated, and he licked his lips as he dropped his jeans to the floor. "Confident and sassy. I like it."

"Then come and get it."

Grinning, he reached for her, and she dodged his advance. He tried again, and she giggled, jumping just out of his grasp. He chuckled. "You get me nearly naked, and *then* you play hard to get?"

"I can't make it easy on you."

"Oh, you're definitely making it hard." He slipped his boxer briefs down his legs, and his dick sprang out at full attention. Yep, she'd made it hard alright. *Wowzers.*

Her eyes widened, and her mouth watered. "Are, uh… Are all werewolves as endowed as you?"

"It's a common trait."

"I knew it!" Jane had laughed when Sophie insisted werewolves would be better in bed than vampires. Trace's massive dick was proof of that. Now to find out if he knew how to use it.

She slinked toward him, took him in her hand, and gave him two firm strokes. His lids fluttered, and a deep, rumbly "*mmm*" emanated from his throat. With one hand on his shoulder, she leaned toward him, giving his earlobe a lick before whispering, "Hey, wolfman. Catch me if you can."

She darted toward the bedroom, but she didn't make it past the threshold before he caught her around the waist and tossed her onto his shoulder. He slapped her ass, and she gasped as he dropped her on the mattress, covering her body with his and pinning her arms above her head.

His heated gaze softened, and he gently kissed the pale pink scars where his teeth had pierced her skin. "I am so sorry I hurt you."

"Now's your chance to make it up to me."

"I plan to, *cher*. And I'm going to enjoy every second of it." He trailed his lips down her bicep toward her armpit, and her heart nearly stopped beating. A quick glance revealed smooth skin, and she let out a relieved breath. She should have checked herself for random fur patches *before* she got naked in front of him.

His beard tickled as he glided his mouth across her collarbone and down to a nipple. Keeping her wrists bound tightly in one hand, he cupped her other breast, teasing her sensitive flesh, hardening her nipples into pearls.

"Damn, you're good with your tongue." Her voice sounded breathy.

His chuckle vibrated across her chest. "You ain't seen nothing yet, sweetheart."

He worked his way down her body, not releasing her

hands until he had to in order to reach her sweet spot, and Lord have mercy, he wasn't kidding. The man knew how to lick. At this rate, it wouldn't take him long to get to the center of her Tootsie Pop.

His warm velvet tongue stroked her clit, building enough pressure in her core to crumble a levee. As he slipped a finger inside her, she lost it. The orgasm crashed into her, tearing her world apart and putting it back together with magical superglue that would never break its hold.

She gripped his shoulders, digging her nails into his skin as she rode the tidal wave to its finish. "Oh, God."

He rose onto his elbows, grinning. "You can call me Trace."

She panted, trying to get her breathing under control. "Jesus."

"Really, Trace will do." He climbed on top of her, pressing kisses to her stomach and between her breasts along the way. "Are you on birth control?"

"Of course." She reached between them, taking his rock-hard dick in her hand. She couldn't wait to have this thing inside her. He put Big Blue to shame.

"Werewolves are immune to disease, but I've got a condom in my pants pocket if you want to use one."

*Oh, hell no.* If they waited any longer she might explode. Wrapping her legs around his waist, she guided him to her center. "It sounds like we're good to go."

His gaze grew so heated, he could have set the bed on fire, and as he pushed inside her, lightning zipped through her body, electrifying her heart. He started out slowly, taking his time to slide all the way out until only his tip remained, before taking her again, his moans saying he relished every delicious inch.

But it wasn't long before his passion overtook him. His thrusts became shorter and faster, and as he tilted his hips, he hit the bullseye...over and over until she screamed his name along with every expletive in her vocabulary.

He spasmed inside her and collapsed with the sexiest male groan she'd ever heard. Sliding his arms beneath her, he hugged her tight, nuzzling into her neck, his breath warm on her skin. His lips grazed her jaw before he nipped her earlobe, sending warm shivers cascading down her spine and through her limbs.

She untangled her legs from around his waist and released her death grip from his shoulders, but he didn't roll off her. Instead, he hugged her even tighter, pressing himself into her as a low growl rumbled in his chest.

Sophie didn't know a lot about werewolves, but the way he held her, the possessive noises emanating from his body, she imagined this might be what it would feel like if he claimed her. She bit her lip to fight her smile as a thousand butterflies flitted from her stomach to her chest. A girl could hope.

"You were good in my dreams, but my imagination did not do you justice."

He lifted his head to look at her, a satisfied grin curving his lips. "Oh, yeah?"

"The real thing is *so* much better. I could do this every night."

His expression smoldered. "Nothing would make me happier than to end my days with you wrapped in my arms. Preferably naked." He moved slightly, resting his hip on the mattress but keeping his leg draped over her, pulling her tight against his body.

Staking his claim. Her stomach fluttered again.

Closing her eyes, she lost herself to the warmth and

strength of Trace's embrace and drifted to sleep. Sometime later, the feeling of tiny paws prancing across the mattress stirred her from her dreams. She opened her eyes to find Crimson's familiar staring into Trace's face.

"Shoo, Jax. Leave him alone." She waved her hand in the cat's direction, but he responded by swatting at Trace's nose.

With a deep, sexy, sleepy inhale, Trace woke, blinking his eyes rapidly at the cat before shooting up in bed. "Jackson? Holy shit. Is that you?"

CHAPTER TEN

Trace wiped the sleep from his eyes and stared into the feline's face. He thought a trivial amount of werewolf magic floated in the air in Sophie's apartment last night, but he'd grown so used to the way his own magic tainting her blood added a slight earthy tone to the warm aroma that he'd dismissed it as coming from her bite.

Now, looking into the intelligent yellow eyes of this supposed familiar, he recognized the faint, muddled scent. He focused his thoughts, sending them to his friend's mind. *"What happened? Did Sophie do this to you?"*

Sophie. He glanced at the beautiful blonde sitting next to him in bed. Her hair, mussed on one side from sleep, flowed over her bare shoulders, and as her blue eyes darted from him to the cat, his heart ached. Trace had fallen for her, hook, line, and sinker, trusting her when she proclaimed her innocence.

It appeared he'd bedded the enemy yet again. This time, no spells were involved though. He'd wedged himself into this fiasco all on his own.

Jackson's muffled voice registered in his mind. *"Communication. Hard. Stuck."*

"You've got to be kidding me." How could he have been so stupid? She was an unregistered witch. He knew better. *Damn it.* He knew better, but he let his dick take the lead anyway. Then his heart followed, and...

"Wait. The cat is your friend?" Sophie slid out of bed and put on a blue silk robe, cinching it at her waist. "I'm confused."

"You've had him all along." He fisted the sheets in his hands, his emotions waging a war in his chest. He didn't want to believe it. That his sweet Sophie could be conniving enough to seduce him while she had Jackson in her clutches the whole time.

"That's Crimson's familiar. I told you I'm cat-sitting." An incredulous look lifted her brow. "It's a cat. It's not..." Her lips parted on a quick inhale. "Jax is short for Jackson. Trace, you have to know I had nothing to do with this."

Didn't she, though?

No, he wouldn't believe it. He couldn't. He knew Sophie, and she was the nicest, most loving person he'd ever met. *Shit.* But the evidence was right in front of him, staring him in the face. And the curse... He'd been in the French Quarter way more than he should lately, always with Sophie, and the force-shift hadn't hit him once. How could it, when the witch responsible for the spell was right beside him?

"The evidence is pretty damn incriminating." Tossing the sheets aside, he slid out of bed and stomped into the living room to retrieve his clothes.

"Are you seriously accusing me of turning your friend into a cat?" Sophie followed on his heels. "After everything we've been through... I helped you steal information from the witches. I poured my heart out to you, letting you know everything about me, and Trace, you *do* know everything. I didn't lie."

He shoved his legs into his jeans and snatched his shirt from the floor. "Really? Okay, let's say you didn't lie. Your friend named her *familiar* Jax, and you didn't make the connection?"

"Why on Earth would I think a cat was your *werewolf* friend?" Sophie crossed her arms and tapped her foot. "I'm sorry for being clueless about how magic works, but you're being clueless about how relationships work. You accused me once, and I let it slide because you didn't know me. Now you do, so I want you to think long and hard before you utter another word, mister. And, no, I am not talking about your dick."

Trace ground his teeth as Jackson jumped onto the back of the couch and rubbed his head against Sophie's leg. She was right. He *did* know her, and the Sophie he was falling head over tail for would never do something like this. Even if she would, she didn't know how.

Scooping Jax into her arms, she nuzzled him, holding him against her chest as she stroked his fur. If the bastard could have smirked, he would have. Instead, he looked at Trace, let out a garbled meow that sounded way too much like a laugh, and rubbed his face between her breasts. *Asshole.*

"You do realize his natural form is a man. He's about six feet tall, dark hair, muscles. And he's practically motorboating you."

Sophie gasped and dropped him on the couch. "Gross. I've been peeing with the door open."

Trace laughed as Jackson's voice sounded in his mind, *"Not Sophie."*

"Thanks, buddy. I figured that out, though you could have saved me the groveling I'm about to do by telling me from the get-go."

"Is he talking to you?" Sophie asked.

"Same way I talked to you last night. I guess he didn't realize you could hear us, or he might have tried." He looked at Jackson, who shook his head. "Sophie, I'm sorry. My brain jumped to a conclusion that my heart tried to fight tooth and claw. I know you wouldn't do something like this, and I don't know why I accused you. Can you ever forgive me?"

She pursed her lips, narrowing her eyes as she drummed her fingers against her biceps. "Damn, you're good at apologies. Fine, I forgive you."

He opened his arms, and she stepped right into his embrace like she belonged there. Hell, they belonged *together.*

"Crimson doesn't seem like a wicked witch." Her breath tickled his neck as she spoke. "I really thought we were becoming friends."

*"Accident. Not wicked,"* Jackson thought-spoke into Trace's mind.

"She might not be bad. We need to confront her and find out exactly what's going on."

"She should be home within the hour. We can meet her upstairs." She glanced at Jax. "He must have recognized you when you came in last night. I wonder why he didn't say anything then?"

*"Didn't want. Mess up. Game."*

Trace chuckled. *"This woman isn't a game. She's the real deal."* He kissed Sophie's cheek. "He didn't want to interrupt us."

"How thoughtful of him. I'll get dressed, and we can

go up and wait for Crimson." Sophie pulled from his embrace, and Jax darted into the bedroom.

He pawed at the bathroom door, pulling it open before jumping onto the counter and letting out a low meow.

Trace followed as Sophie stopped at her dresser for some clothes. "I'm not good with cat-speak, man. Can you send me your thoughts?"

Rising onto his back paws, Jackson swiped at the medicine cabinet, trying to pull it open.

"You need something from in there?" He tugged on the corner of the mirror, and it swung open. Jackson grabbed a wad of toilet paper in his mouth and set it on the counter, nosing it toward Trace.

"Are you hiding something in here?" he called through the doorway to Sophie. "Something wrapped up in toilet paper has Jax's attention."

He unrolled the paper as Sophie shouted, "No!" She darted through the door, but it was too late. He'd already seen the contents.

"This is fur." His mind scrambled to understand what he was looking at. "Where did you...? Did this come from...? What the hell, Sophie?"

Chewing her bottom lip, she glanced from Jackson to Trace. "Yes, it's fur. It came from me." She lowered her gaze, and the tips of her ears reddened.

"You? But you said you didn't—"

"I lied, okay? It only happened once, so after a while, I didn't think anything of it. I forgot it was even in there. I don't know why I kept it."

The corners of his mouth twitched, and hope bloomed in his chest. "So, you are showing signs of the mutation.

There's a chance you might become a werewolf at the next full moon."

She shrugged. "Yeah. I mean, I guess so. Why are you smiling?"

"I would love for you to become a werewolf. That's not why I bit you, of course, but Sophie, I'm falling for you hard. Werewolves are allowed to mate with any species, but there are so many benefits to mating with another were. Especially another red wolf."

Her mouth opened, the words seeming to get stuck in her throat. *Shit.* He spent one night with the woman, and he was already talking about becoming mates. He was seriously off his game. "I'm sorry. I shouldn't have mentioned the mating bit. It's way too soon for that."

"No. It's…" She shook her head, a smile lighting on her lips. "I'm glad to know you feel that way. I'm falling for you too."

His breath came out in a gush of relief, and he stepped toward her, opening his arms.

She held up her hands and stepped back. "But you have to understand that I am not going to become a werewolf. The fur thing has only happened once, and I'm not showing any other signs. I'm a witch, Trace, and if Crimson can't unlock my magic, I'll find someone else who can. It's my destiny."

He dropped his arms to his sides. Maybe her heightened sense of smell and her above-average hearing had nothing to do with his magic running through her veins. If she really thought this one instance of fur was the only sign she'd shown, maybe she wasn't going to become a werewolf after all.

"I understand." She didn't want to be like him.

"Do you still want me, even if I never become a wolf?" For the first time, uncertainty flashed in her eyes.

"Of course." The question was, would she still want him when she became a full witch?

---

Sophie clutched her grandmother's grimoire to her chest and led the way up the stairs to Crimson's apartment. Her instinct had been to carry Jax, but Trace's reminder that there was a full-grown man inside that little kitty body meant the so-called familiar could walk it.

What was it with shifters pretending to be house pets around her? Between giving Trace a bath and letting Jax curl up on her chest, she was about ready to be done with animals altogether. Or at least until she could spot magic with her own nose and eyes.

"Now, before you go accusing her of nefarious acts, let her explain, okay?" She unlocked the door, and Jax darted between her legs into the apartment.

Trace huffed. "She turned my best friend into a cat; she lied under oath to her coven. She's got a lot of explaining to do."

They stepped into the loft area and found Jax sitting beneath the giant portrait of a man. "That's Jackson." Trace stepped toward the painting, rubbing his beard as he admired Crimson's work. "Did she paint this?"

Sophie started to answer, but he was looking at the cat. Instead, she sank onto the couch and opened the grimoire to her grandmother's prophecy.

"Why didn't you come to the pack for help? Or to me?" Trace followed Jax into the seating area and sat on the sofa next to Sophie.

"What did he say?" she asked.

"Whatever spell he's under is making it hard for him to communicate. All I got was 'embarrassed.'"

"Hmm. I can see why he'd be embarrassed with the way you talk about cats. I wouldn't want you to know if it happened to me."

"Like you didn't want me to know about the fur incident?"

"I told you that happened shortly after you bit me. I didn't trust you yet."

"But you trust me now?"

She placed a hand on his thigh and squeezed. Damn, this man was muscular. "I do."

"Will you tell me if anything else like that happens? I want to be prepared. If we can't get this mess sorted out, I'll either need to protect you or run away with you somewhere safe."

"I'm not running away." She moved the book in her lap to rest against his leg. "Look, I want to show you something. This is a prophecy my grandmother wrote about me shortly after my dad was born."

She ran her finger over the four lines of text as Trace read the words. "Jane helped me figure it out, and it makes so much sense. The land where the Spanish reigned is obviously New Orleans. Man turning beast is you, and what's done will be undone means I'm not going to turn into a werewolf."

He made a noncommittal sound in his throat and tapped the page. "I don't like that last line, 'All must be lost to find everything.' It doesn't sound good."

"I think it's already happened. I was about ready to pack it up and go back to Texas before I found this. It gave me hope, and I'm still here, finding magic." She took his hand. "And a man to make my dreams come true."

"Sophie, I—" He cocked his head. "Footsteps on the stairs. She's home." He shot to his feet and strode toward the door.

"What are you going to do? Ambush her?" She closed the book and set it on the coffee table.

"If she sees me sitting on the couch when she opens the door, she's likely to tuck tail and run. There's a reason she doesn't want anyone to know what she did to Jackson." He leaned his back against the wall, and as the door swung open, it concealed him from Crimson's view.

Crimson stopped in the entry and set her suitcase on the floor. "Hey, Sophie. You didn't have to bring Jax home. I would've come down and gotten him."

Sophie cringed. "We need to talk."

"We *all* need to talk." Trace kicked the door shut and stood in front of it, crossing his arms and flexing his muscles in an oh so masculine way. If he wasn't trying to be threatening to her friend, Sophie's mouth might have watered at his sex appeal.

Okay, her mouth watered anyway.

"Umm…" Crimson froze, her gaze darting from Sophie to Jax to Trace and back to Sophie. "See, this is why I told you not to let him around any other supes. With the pack involved, it's going to screw up everything."

"The pack isn't involved yet." Sophie scooted to the edge of the couch and patted a cushion. "I convinced Trace to listen to your explanation before he reports you."

"How very kind of you." Crimson gave Trace a once-over before strutting to the sofa and perching on the edge like she was ready to bolt.

Sophie couldn't blame her. Trace exuded enough testosterone to make Chuck Norris tremble.

"Oh, good. You brought your grimoire." Crimson ran a hand over the cover of the book. "We can fix this together. If my mom hadn't fallen, we'd have already fixed it. I'm a master at channeling magic."

"How is your mom?" Sophie mentally smacked herself upside the head. Even in a crisis, she could show some manners.

"She's good. Has my dad waiting on her hand and foot. Now that the worst of the pain has subsided, I think they're both enjoying it a little."

Trace cleared his throat as he dropped into a chair across from them. "Can we focus, ladies? What did you do to Jackson?"

"I turned him into a familiar, obviously." Crimson rolled her eyes and smirked at Sophie.

Biting her bottom lip, Sophie shook her head. She and Trace could talk in circles before getting to the point of a conversation, but she could tell his patience had worn as thin as a sheet of single-ply toilet paper.

"It was an accident." Crimson cast her gaze to Jackson, who sat on the arm of an accent chair, flicking his tail. "If Jax could talk, he'd tell you himself."

"He did." Sophie patted her hand. "He told Trace a little with their thought-talking magic, but he's having a hard time communicating. We need you to fill in the blanks."

Crimson nodded and glanced at Trace. "Do you swear you haven't reported it? My magic is at stake."

"I know," he said. "You lied to your high priestess under oath. They'll bind your magic permanently for that offense."

"They'll bind my powers regardless if I can't fix this. I'm on my last strike." Crimson's shoulders slumped, her mask of confidence slipping off, raw vulnerability replacing it. "I was hoping to talk to Sophie about this alone. It's rather embarrassing for us both, isn't it, Jax?"

A deep mewl sounded from Jax's throat, and he hopped onto the sofa next to Crimson, placing a paw on her leg in comfort.

"I'm sorry, Jax." She rested her hand on his back. "It was a role-playing thing we were doing. I screwed up a sex game."

Trace's eyebrows shot up, and Sophie bit the inside of her cheek.

Crimson let out a dry laugh. "It was a fantasy, you know? The wicked witch turns her familiar human and has her way with him." She paused, cutting her gaze between the two of them. "Oh, like neither of you has ever done anything kinky in the bedroom. Don't judge."

Sophie held up her hands. "I'm not judging."

"Anyway, I had to turn him into a familiar first, before I turned him into human form again. Making him a cat was easy. Undoing the spell turned out to be a problem."

Sophie scrunched her brow. "Why didn't you let him shift into wolf form and just pretend you turned him back?"

"No witch has a wolf as a familiar. Cats, ferrets, Guinea pigs, those are all possible. The closest to a wolf would be a fox, and those are extremely rare." She shrugged. "We were trying to be realistic."

Trace rubbed his beard. "And you agreed to this, Jax?" He nodded, an incredulous look widening his eyes. "He says he did, but why didn't you come to the pack for help? We could have kept it quiet."

"Look at him," Crimson said. "He's a *cat*. If his pack-mates saw him in this state, they'd never let him live it down. I'm sure he wasn't thrilled for you to find out either."

Trace crossed his arms. "We all make mistakes. Your secret's safe with me."

"I've tried turning him back many, many times, but it's not working. I must've done something wrong in the original spell to turn him into a cat, and now I can't undo it on my own. I need the help of a fauna witch." She looked at Sophie.

"Surely there are other fauna witches in the coven, right?"

"There's one, but I can't go to the coven for help. This really is my last strike. I've screwed up too many spells, and the high priestess told me, point blank, if I screwed up again, my magic would be bound for life. She's going to turn me human."

"Oh, no. We can't have that." Sophie had only known about the existence of magic for less than a year, and she couldn't imagine having it all taken away from her now. Crimson had been a witch her whole life. She couldn't let her friend lose her powers. "How can I help?"

"If I can channel your magic, I'm sure I can do it. Right now, *something* happens with every transformation spell I try, but it doesn't affect Jax. My magic is strong, but it's wild. I can't seem to focus it into him in the right place."

Trace straightened his spine. "How many times have you tried to change him back?"

Crimson counted on her fingers. "Half a dozen at least."

His jaw ticked as his hands curled into fists in his lap. "And how long have you been out of town?"

She shrugged. "A few days."

He looked at Sophie, and the realization hit her square between the eyes. "The force-shifts," they said in unison.

"Every time you cast a spell to change him back," Trace said, "you send out a wave of magic that forces any red wolf within a two-mile radius of you to shift against their will. My pack has been banned from entering the French Quarter while I investigate."

Crimson's jaw fell slack. "I... Damn."

"Damn indeed." Trace stood and paced the length of the coffee table. "We were about to start a war."

"Oh, no. We need to fix this," Crimson said.

"I need to report this to my Alpha." Trace pulled his phone from his pocket, and Jackson hissed before darting toward him and swiping a paw at his leg.

"No, Trace. Please." Sophie padded to him and grasped his forearm before he could dial the number. "She'll lose her powers."

"That's not my problem."

"What if it were you? What if you could never shift again? How would that make you feel? We can help her. I know we can."

His dark honey eyes held hers, and she could almost feel his resolution dissolving. The tension in his muscles eased as he lowered his phone to his pocket and laughed dryly. "The power you have over me is witchcraft."

"I promise I'm not doing a thing to force you."

"She tames your beast." Crimson stood and strutted toward them. "Your primal fight or flight instinct is tempered when she's near, forcing you to think rationally before acting." She winked at Sophie. "In other words, she's good for you."

"Don't I know it." His gaze heated as he swept it over Sophie, lighting her nerves on fire without even the slightest touch. He was good for her too.

He looked at Crimson. "I assume you have a plan then?"

"May I?" She gestured to the grimoire.

"Of course." Sophie followed her to the sofa and sank down next to her as she flipped through the pages, nodding and making *mmm* and *ahh* noises as she understood a hundred times more than Sophie did when she tried to decipher it.

Trace sat next to Sophie, his thigh pressing into hers, and he took her hand. His touch reassured her, sending the message that he intended to go along with whatever plan Crimson cooked up.

"Your grandmother was a fauna witch as well, though that's not surprising." She closed the book and smiled. "She was powerful too, which means you will be as well… once we unlock your magic."

Sophie's quick intake of air made her cough, and as she tried to speak, the coughing worsened until her eyes watered.

"Are you okay?" Trace rubbed her back as she gasped for air.

"Fine." Two more coughs, and she could breathe again. "Just choking on my own spit. I'm talented like that." She rested a hand on Trace's thigh and turned to Crimson. "You can unlock my powers? You can make me a real witch?" Excitement bubbled in her chest, making her giddy. This was it. Her dreams were finally going to come true.

Crimson pressed her lips together and shook her head. "I can't release your magic. It's sealed with a lock only your grandmother can undo."

And there went all the excitement, fizzing out like a can of soda that was shaken before it was opened. An exhilarating explosion followed by an empty container. She slumped into Trace's side. "My grandmother is dead."

A mischievous smile curved Crimson's lips. "Then we'll just have to bring her back to life."

CHAPTER ELEVEN

Sophie's hand was cold and damp in Trace's palm as he guided her down the corridor. His boots thudded on the tiles, echoing off the plain white walls, while the swarm of vampires behind them barely made a sound.

Maybe it wasn't a swarm per se, but Sophie had insisted on bringing every supe she knew along on this excursion to resurrect a sixty-years-dead witch from beyond the grave. Crimson brought up the rear of the group with Jax tucked inside the backpack slung over her right shoulder. Weren't they a motley crew?

Trace got it, though. These people were Sophie's pack. She may have thought she never belonged anywhere, but he could almost feel the concern emanating from her vampire friends as they followed her down the hall. She'd found her home, if only she could recognize it.

"Do we have to do this in a morgue?" Sophie's hushed voice trembled as he opened the door and motioned for her to go through.

"She's a necromancer. This is where she works." He led the way to the third door on the left and knocked.

"Hi, Trace." Jasmine smiled as she opened the door. Her long, black hair was tied back in a twist, and she wore a white lab coat over tan slacks and a navy shirt. "You must be Sophie. I'm Jasmine Lee, resident necromancer and research assistant to the coroner."

"Hi." Sophie shook her hand and glanced into the office. A metal desk and computer occupied most of the space, and an old school filing cabinet sat in the back corner, collecting dust. "Are you going to summon my grandma in there? Don't you need candles and crystal balls and stuff?"

Jasmine flashed him a quizzical look. "I thought you said she was a witch?"

"Her grandmother was." He rested a hand on the small of Sophie's back. "Her powers were never unlocked, so this is all new to her."

"Gotcha." She pulled the door shut behind her as she stepped into the hall, and her lip curled. "Oh, you brought vampires. Joy."

Jane fisted her hands on her hips. "What do you have against vampires?"

Jasmine looked her up and down, clearly unimpressed, and Trace held in a chuckle. "You're dead bodies I can't use."

Jane's mouth fell open, and she looked like she was about to argue, but Ethan touched her arm, shaking his head ever so slightly.

"Our bodies are more useful than you can imagine, *ma chère*." Gaston puffed out his chest and gestured toward his hips. "Perhaps you would like to take one for an example excursion? I feel you would reevaluate your opinion if you did."

Ethan cleared his throat. "I think you mean test drive."

Gaston smiled, showing fang. "She knows what I mean."

Trace fought his eye roll, but Jasmine let hers loose and then looked at Sophie. "No, I don't need candles or crystals, but what I do need is a corpse. Follow me to the meat locker."

"A corpse?" Sophie froze, tightening her grip on Trace's hand. "Why do you need a corpse? Can't you just call to her and tell me what she says, or channel her or something like the psychics do on TV?"

Jasmine laughed and motioned for them to follow her. "You have me mistaken for a medium. I can't put a soul into a body that already has one. We need a corpse if you want to talk to your grandma, and unfortunately, your undead friends won't do."

"No. Trace, this isn't right." Sophie pleaded with her eyes. "She can't put my grandma's soul into another person's body. That's gross, and you didn't tell me we were making a zombie. I've seen *The Walking Dead*. I know what zombies do."

"She can," he assured her. "She's not making a zombie, and she does this all the time. Her main job here is to resurrect murder victims to find out who their killers were."

Jasmine held up a finger. "That's my off-the-books job that only the higher-ups know about. Officially, I'm a research assistant."

"Okay, but surely we could use a medium, right? Corpses are icky." She flashed an apologetic look at Jane. "No offense, hon. I'm still getting used to how cold you feel."

"None taken. You're sleeping with an animal. Let's call it even." Jane winked.

"Does your grandma's spirit haunt you?" the necromancer asked.

"Well, no. I don't think so." Sophie shivered, and Trace pulled her to his side. He'd been a bit disgusted the first time he watched Jasmine do her thing for a case he was working. He might have puked in the trash can, but there was no evidence of that. He'd made sure of it.

"Does she haunt your dad?" Jasmine used her ID badge to unlock the door, and it swung open automatically. "Has anyone in your family ever mentioned hearing from her ghost?"

"No."

"Then, chances are, she moved on to the place souls go to rest a long time ago, 'crossed the bridge,' so to speak. Mediums can reach out to spirits who are still hanging around the in-between, that space between the living world and the land of the dead. If you want to pull someone back to this side of the bridge after they've already crossed it, you need a necromancer." She disappeared through the doorway.

"She's right." Crimson adjusted the backpack on her shoulder. "And we need your grandma to work magic while she's here to unlock your powers. She'll need a body for that. Ghosts can't cast spells."

"It'll be okay." Trace clutched her shoulders, looking into her eyes and giving her all the reassurance he could with his gaze. "I'll be here the whole time. You've got Crimson, Jane, Ethan, Gaston. We're all here for you."

She held his gaze for a moment before looking at each of her friends in turn. Then, with a deep inhale—and thank goodness her sense of smell hadn't reached full werewolf strength because the stench of death and antiseptic was enough to make him puke all over again—she straightened her spine and nodded. "Let's do this."

Turning on her heel, Sophie followed the necromancer into the room she called "the meat locker." Two steel tables stood side by side in the center of the room, with massive lighting contraptions hanging above each. Rows of metal doors stacked three high lined two of the walls, and Sophie cringed as she imagined what each one might contain. "It's more like a meat library, don't you think? With everyone filed away in drawers."

Jasmine nodded thoughtfully. "I like it. It's not quite the Dewey Decimal system, but we are pretty organized."

Trace held his fist against his nose, and Sophie could only imagine how pungent the sickly-sweet smells of death and decay mixed with chemicals must have been for him.

"Are you okay?" She put her hand on his elbow. "You look a little green."

"It stinks to high heaven in here." He dropped his arm to his side and swallowed hard.

"There's the trash can, if you need it." Jasmine smirked, and Trace glared in return. Sophie made a mental note to find out what that was about later.

Jax let out a deep whine as Crimson unzipped the backpack, and he jumped onto one of the exam tables before licking his paw.

"We have got to get him turned back into a werewolf," Trace said. "Watching him actually behave like a cat is unnerving."

"That's why we're here." Sophie rubbed Trace's shoulder, and he covered her hand with his.

The door clicked shut behind Gaston, and he turned around, peering through the narrow vertical window. "As much as I love a good corpse raising, I'll volunteer to be lookout. I can glamour anyone who gets too close."

"That probably won't be necessary. This place is dead at night." Jasmine snorted and covered her mouth, laughing at her joke.

Sophie bit her lip. When the others didn't join in the laughter either, Jasmine lifted her hands and dropped them at her sides. "Lighten up. It's just a little morgue humor."

"It was funny," Sophie said. "But my friend's magic is on the line, and this guy might be stuck a cat forever if this doesn't work."

"Gotcha. Serious business. I did tell you to bring something that belonged to the person we're trying to contact, right?" Jasmine asked.

"No, you didn't." Trace crossed his arms.

"Well, shit. I've been working for the police so long, I forget most people don't know how this works. I need something she owned so I can connect with her."

"We have her grimoire. Crimson?" Sophie gestured to the backpack, and Crimson unzipped another pocket. Sophie retrieved the book and offered it to Jasmine. "Will this work?"

"Perfect." Jasmine pulled a dry erase marker from her coat pocket and scribbled a design on the empty table. "This is a vévé. It's a symbol that represents Baron Samedi, the Voodoo spirit of death."

"I didn't know you were a Voodoo practitioner," Trace said.

"I'm not, but I have friends who've taught me a thing or two. I can call a spirit without the Baron's help, but having his blessing makes the process a helluva lot easier." She finished the picture, a decorative cross with two coffins behind it, and placed the grimoire next to it.

Jane moved next to Sophie. "I always pictured stuff like this being done in a cemetery on a foggy night. You're ruining necromancy for me."

"Oh, we could do this in a cemetery," Jasmine said. "But the bodies here are fresh. If you think what we're about to do is gross, imagine doing it with a corpse that's been rotting for who knows how long."

Sophie shuddered. "Here is good."

"There's also the issue of the way New Orleanians bury their dead. Those aboveground tombs essentially cook the remains, turning them to ash over time. Unless you find one that was recently buried, chances are there isn't going to be enough left of the corpse for a spirit to do anything with."

"Well, damn." Jane crossed her arms. "That's no fun."

"I raised you from the dead in a cemetery," Ethan said with a twinkle in his eyes from across the room.

Jane cast a loving gaze toward him as he guarded the door with Gaston. "Yes, you did, my sexy, blood-drinking man candy. You're the best thing that's ever happened to me, and I'll be sure to show Vlad my appreciation as soon as this is done."

"Vlad?" Crimson arched a brow at Sophie.

"She named his dick Vlad because he impales her with it."

Crimson laughed. "Clever. I like her."

"The three of us will have to grab a drink sometime," Jane said.

"I'd love that." Sophie grinned at her friends.

"Ladies, can we focus?" Trace's jaw ticked. "Jax has

been a cat for long enough."

Jane leaned over and whispered in her ear, "Have you named his yet?"

Sophie snickered. "I haven't had time to think of one."

Trace cleared his throat.

Jasmine laughed. "Humor is how we handle all this death." She patted Trace on the shoulder. "I couldn't work here without it. What do you think of this one?" She opened a locker and slid a body out on a platform. "It's the freshest one we've got." She peeled back the sheet to reveal a man in his late fifties.

"Oh, no." Crimson shook her head adamantly. "That's a man."

"Spirit is spirit." Jasmine shrugged. "It doesn't matter the sex of the body."

"What's that on his neck?" Sophie asked.

"Crap. I forgot he had a tracheotomy. That'll make it hard for the ghost to speak through him." Jasmine slid the man back into the drawer and tapped a finger against her lips. "Oh! I know just the one." She opened another locker and revealed an eighty-something-year-old woman with silver hair and pale, paper-thin skin.

Sophie's stomach turned. "That's someone's grandma."

"She's about to be *your* grandma," Jasmine said. "Wait. Is this your first time seeing a dead body?"

Sophie pressed her lips together and nodded.

"A virgin. No wonder." Jasmine laughed and gestured to Trace. "He whined like a little pup the first time he watched me do this."

Trace bristled. "Watch who you call a pup. There's nothing little about me."

"It's true," Sophie said. "He's buried his bone in me. It's massive."

Jasmine blinked. "Have you heard of the expression TMI?" Shaking her head, she turned and placed one hand on the grimoire, the other on the dead woman's forehead, and began chanting in a language Sophie didn't understand.

The energy in the air thickened, and Sophie's arm hairs stood on end as Jasmine quieted. Utter silence filled the room for a good twenty seconds before Jasmine pressed her palms together and bowed at the design she'd drawn on the table.

"Voila." She gestured toward the corpse, and its eyes blinked open.

Jane clutched Sophie's hand. "Holy mother of goat cheese pizza! It worked."

The corpse's brow furrowed as it glanced around the room. Lifting its arms in front of its face, it flipped its hands over and back before slowly rising to a sitting position. "Wha—" The corpse cleared its throat. "What in the name of the goddess happened to my body?"

Sophie gasped, her head spinning as Trace gripped her arm and held her upright.

"It's not your body, ma'am," Jasmine said. "You're just borrowing it for a bit. Can you tell me your name?"

The woman tilted her head, cracking her neck. "It's Maggie Burroughs. You know that. You're the one who called me." Her gaze landed on the book. "Oh! Is that my grimoire?" She eased herself off the table, and the sheet that was covering her pooled on the floor as she waddled toward the book. Her boobs sagged down almost to her waist, and her skin had so many wrinkles, it looked like crepe paper.

Sophie sighed. She was not looking forward to old age.

Trace cleared his throat, and Jasmine grabbed the

sheet, wrapping it around the woman's body and tying it at her back. With the corpse properly covered, Sophie spoke to the woman. "Grandma?"

"Who are you calling grandma? The last age I remember being was twenty-five." She wiggled her fingers. "These are not the hands of a twenty-five-year-old. I'm not the soul who belongs in this body."

"I know." Sophie touched her frigid, lifeless hand, and jerked away. Nope, she'd never get used to the feeling of cold flesh. "You're my dad's mother."

Maggie tilted her head, holding Sophie's gaze. "My baby, Mark? He had a daughter?"

"Yes, ma'am."

Maggie looked around the room at all the people staring at her. "Vampires. A witch. A werewolf. Oh, you must be a fauna witch like me," she said to Sophie. "We have a weakness for shifters, and you found yourself a sexy one." She wiggled her old lady eyebrows at Trace, and he tensed.

Sophie couldn't help but laugh. "Wait. Was Grandpa…?"

"I had a weakness for shifters, but I fell in love with a human." She reached a hand to Sophie's face, but she pulled away. Maggie looked at her fingers. "This body is a little wrinkly, isn't it? Cold too. Why am I wearing this horrid outfit again?"

"I need your help. Since you died before I was born, my powers were never unlocked. I need you to release them."

She shook her head sadly. "Oh, honey, I would, but I can't train you. I can already feel my attachment to this body slipping, and an untrained witch is a dangerous witch."

"I'll train her." Crimson stood next to Sophie. "We're neighbors and good friends. I'll teach her everything she needs to know."

"That's an awful big undertaking."

"Please." Crimson clasped her hands together. "If you can't unbind her powers, can you at least help me change him back?" She picked up Jax and held him toward Maggie.

"Oh, my. Is that a werewolf?" She placed a hand on Jax's head, and he froze. "What did you do to him, child?"

"I messed up." Crimson explained the entire ordeal. "If I can't change him back, I'll lose my powers. The red wolves will start a war with the witches. The supernatural balance in New Orleans will fall apart, and it will be all my fault. I'm a bad witch."

"I see." Maggie looked at Sophie and then at Jax. "I can't change him back. That will require spell work I simply don't have time to conjure, and I'm afraid only a fauna witch can reverse this spell."

"What about me then?" Sophie pleaded. "If you unbind my magic, Crimson can channel it. We can save Jax together."

"You can channel?" She reached for Crimson's face. "Pardon my cold skin, but I need to touch you to properly read your magic." Cupping Crimson's cheek, she closed her eyes and nodded. "It seems that's the only way to save your friend. When is the next full moon?"

"In two days," Trace said.

"That doesn't give you much time. Sophie, my dear, sweet heir." She gasped. "My heir." Gripping the grimoire, she opened it to the prophecy and read the lines. "What's done will be undone. Goddess, could I be any more cryptic when I wrote that? It should be 'What's bound will be unbound.' I believe I was talking about your powers, dear. Come." She motioned for Sophie to come closer.

Sophie swallowed hard, willing herself to approach her grandmother wrapped in a corpse, and as the old woman reached for her face, she held her breath. The cold, dead hands cupped her cheeks, and she swallowed the sour taste from her mouth.

"Oh, dear. Now I see. I wasn't sure when I wrote this, but…" She dropped her arms to her sides. "You've been bitten, and the only thing stopping you from transforming into a werewolf at the next full moon is the fact that your powers are bound. If I unbind them now, you'll have the magic of a witch for two days. At midnight on the night of the full moon, all but your inborn power will dissolve as you transform."

"I'll lose my magic?" Sophie's lower lip trembled, so she bit it.

"I'm afraid so," Maggie said.

"But I… It's my destiny. I'm supposed to be a witch." A spark of anger ignited in her chest. It was irrational. She knew that, but there she was, getting mad at Trace for an accident. He didn't mean to bite her, and if she thought about it, the bite was just as much her fault as it was his. She should have known not to put her hand in an unknown animal's face, especially at a supernatural night club.

"I'm so sorry, Sophie." As Trace reached for her, he let his hand fall to his side.

She swallowed the thickness from her throat and fought the tears collecting on her lower lids. "What if we wait until after the full moon? Can we call you back here in a couple of days and do it then?"

"That'll cost extra." Jasmine leaned a hip against the table.

"I'll cover the fee," Jane said. "Might as well make myself *useful*." She glared at the necromancer.

Maggie shook her head. "I'm afraid if you want to save your werewolf friend, that won't be possible. The spell Crimson used to change him will become permanent at the full moon."

"He'll be a cat forever?" Sophie asked.

"That's what permanent means, dear."

"Crimson!" Sophie scolded her friend, backhanding her on the arm. "What were you thinking?"

Crimson raised her hands. "I know I screwed up. Like I said, I'm a bad witch."

"No." Sophie shook her head. "I can't do that to Jax. If I have to lose my powers to fix this, so be it."

"Sophie," Trace mumbled, but what more could he say? If she didn't do this, his best friend would be a cat forever. A war would break out. Talk about never fitting in anywhere again. She'd never forgive herself if supernatural New Orleans went to shit when she had the power to save it.

She looked at her grandmother. "I'll do it. Please unbind my magic."

"Isn't there anything else we can do?" Jane asked. "Would biting her help? Maybe some vampire blood or our magical healing saliva? I licked her wound right after Trace bit her. Maybe I need to lick her again?"

Gaston lifted a hand. "I volunteer to lick her from head to toe."

Trace stiffened, and Sophie put a hand on his chest to calm him. "Thank you, Gaston, but that won't be necessary."

He shrugged. "Anything to help you keep your magic, dear friend."

Jane rolled her eyes. "And I thought chivalry was dead."

"You have good friends." Maggie attempted a smile, but only one side of the corpse's face lifted. "There is something you could do, though it will be expensive."

"Name your price," Jane said. "Money is no object when it comes to my BFF and her happiness."

"It's not my price, dear," Maggie said. "You'll need a spell that only a special high priestess can cast. It requires the power of three, so she'll need the help of her two strongest witches. It's called a *hechizo anular*, but with only two days to cast, I'm not sure they could create the potion in time." She looked at Crimson. "I know of two witches in existence who have the power to create the potion. I was one of them. You can ask your priestess if she knows of another nearby."

Crimson swallowed hard and lowered her gaze to the floor.

"We can't ask the priestess," Sophie said. "This whole ordeal is under the coven's radar, lest we start a war."

"Who is the other priestess who can do it?" Jane asked.

"Her name is Kathleen Simmons," Maggie replied. "Last I knew, she ran the Austin, Texas, coven. She was the high priestess over the entire state."

Crimson nodded. "She's still there. I recognize the name."

"Texas?" Jane pulled Sophie into a tight hug. "I got this. Get your magic unlocked, and I'll see you again in two days." She released Sophie and hugged Trace. "Take care of her while I'm gone."

"Always," Trace said.

"Gaston, how fast can your Maserati get us to Texas? It's time to put my Governor's daughter status to good use."

Gaston smiled. "The Fast and Feverous have nothing on me."

"It's *The Fast and the Furious*," Ethan said. "It's… Never mind. Let's go."

Ethan and Gaston stepped through the door, and Maggie tugged the sheet, letting it fall to the floor. Trace stared at his shoes, and Jane paused in the doorway. "Sky-clad?" she asked.

"It's the best way to work this kind of magic."

"You're just like I imagined." Jane giggled as she slipped through the door.

Maggie borrowed a pen from Jasmine and wrote her final spell on the next blank page of the grimoire. "This potion takes two days to make, so you'll need to start it tonight. Then, the incantation must be cast on the night of the full moon for full potency, as close to midnight as possible, but it must be before the clock strikes twelve, or our friend's condition will be permanent."

Crimson scanned the spell and nodded. "Got it. We can do this."

"Once the spell on Jax has been reversed, then you must drink the potion Jane brings you before midnight as well. If you don't, you will transform into a werewolf and lose your magic forever. Are you ready?"

Sophie nodded.

"Wait. You don't have to do this." Trace touched Sophie's arm and looked at Jax. "Jackson says he doesn't want to be the reason you lose your magic. We can figure something else out."

"No. I have to do this." She patted his hand and turned to her grandmother. "I'm ready."

Placing her hands on either side of Sophie's head, Maggie whispered a spell. Her cold touch was replaced with a warm, tingling sensation that spread through Sophie's body from the top of her head to the tips of her toes. As her grandmother released her hold, the feeling subsided, and something in Sophie's core popped.

A fiery sensation rolled up from her stomach to her throat, singeing her esophagus before the heat spread across her chest and dissipated. She'd expected getting her magic unlocked to feel, well…magical. Instead, it felt like a bad case of heartburn. "That's it? I'm a witch now?"

Maggie nodded. "Indeed you are, my dear. I'm sorry I wasn't there to bring you up in magic, but I'm happy I got to meet you now."

"Me too." Sophie fought the urge to hug the corpse containing her grandmother's spirit.

"Now, where's the necromancer?" Maggie spun around and stumbled, catching herself on the edge of the table.

"Here." Jasmine padded toward her.

"Please get me out of this awful skin before I die all over again. I much prefer the freedom of being made of pure energy."

"Bye, Grandma." Sophie waved as Jasmine guided Maggie back to the shelf.

"This part can get a little icky, what with the seizures and all." Jasmine waved toward the door. "I'll send you a bill."

"Let's go get your magic on." Crimson grinned and stuffed Jax into the backpack.

Trace pressed his lips into a hard line and nodded before following them out the door.

CHAPTER TWELVE

Trace sat in a white microfiber chair in Crimson's loft and watched Sophie in the kitchen with the witch, learning how to cast spells. Correction: they were both witches now, at least until midnight tonight.

Sophie had swept her long, blonde hair into a high ponytail, and the excitement in her eyes made Trace's chest ache. Crimson handed her an apron with *Life's a Witch* embroidered on the front, and Sophie caught his gaze before spinning in a circle and gesturing to the cloth. "What do you think?"

"Witchcraft looks good on you." Hell, anything looked good on her, and despite his selfish desire for Jane *not* to get the potion to neutralize his magic in Sophie, her happiness was the most important thing. Never mind the fact that they'd both stop aging if she became a werewolf and they mated. Their strength would double, they'd live several hundred years, and they could help to repopulate the pack with full-blooded red wolves.

Those things didn't matter because he never should have bitten her in the first place. If Jane didn't obtain the potion in time, Trace would get his selfish wish, but at the cost of Sophie's happiness.

"Any word from Jane?" he asked.

Sophie glanced at the clock. "Not since you asked me two hours ago. It's daylight. She's dead right now."

Damn vampires and their stupid weakness. He should have sent someone from his pack to get the potion. Someone who could function any time of day.

Sophie repeated a rhyming spell and sprinkled dark red powder into a copper bowl. The concoction she was mixing sparked, and steam rose from the container, making her jump and then giggle. "Did it work?"

Crimson poured the liquid into a small glass bottle. "It did. You're a natural."

"You hear that, babe?" She took off the apron and laid it on the counter. "I'm a natural."

"I heard."

"All right," Crimson said. "We've got the potion, and darkness falls in two hours. You two head home and give me some time to get in the zone. I'll meet you in the designated spot at ten. Jax, are you going with them or staying?"

Jackson slinked into the kitchen and jumped onto the counter next to Crimson. He'd either forgiven the witch, or he could sense Trace's mood and wanted to give him some alone time with Sophie.

"Sounds good." Sophie took his hand and led him downstairs to her apartment.

They settled on the couch, and he gazed at the beautiful witch he'd fallen in love with. Magic now glowed in her aura, and her intoxicating cinnamon scent grew deeper, stronger. She laced her fingers through his, her grin lighting up her entire face.

"Have I told you how beautiful your smile is?" he asked.

"Maybe once or twice." She pressed her lips to his cheek, lingering near his skin as she inhaled deeply. "*Mmm...* You've always had an amazing scent, but now that I can smell your magic, it's hard to keep my hands off you." She climbed into his lap, straddling him.

"Who says you have to keep them off?"

She sat back, resting her hands on his chest, the warmth of her fingers through his shirt making him wish there was no fabric between them at all. Her eyes searched his, and she tilted her head. "I'm happy, Trace. I know this spell is going to fix Jackson, and I've suddenly found myself with everything I've ever wanted within my grasp."

"What if Jane doesn't make it back with the potion in time? What if midnight comes and goes, and you turn into a werewolf?" She could lose it all because of him.

"She'll make it. Jane always pulls through."

"But what if she doesn't?"

"She will." She slipped her hands beneath his shirt, the skin on skin contact tightening his stomach. "And after all this is done, we're going to come back here and celebrate. A witch and her werewolf, together..." Her teeth grazed her bottom lip.

He took her face in his hands, stroking his thumbs across her cheeks. "Forever?"

She lowered her gaze before blinking up at him. "I hope so."

"No matter what happens? Even if...?"

"No ifs. It's all going to work out. You'll see."

He did see. Her refusal to even entertain the idea that she might be a werewolf by midnight sat heavy in his stomach like a brick of his grandmother's week-old meatloaf. Arguing with her now wouldn't do any good, though. Whatever was going to happen would happen, so he might as well enjoy the moment.

He winked. "Just promise you'll never try to turn me into a cat?"

"Why on Earth would I do that when I can have all this?" She roamed her hands over his chest and down his stomach, popping the button on his jeans. "We have a few hours before we have to meet Crimson and Jax. How about a little pre-celebration?"

"I suppose I'm up for a party."

She slid down his zipper and reached into his pants, smiling wickedly. "You certainly are."

The feel of her soft fingers wrapped around his rock-hard dick made his eyelids flutter, and as she rose to her feet, undressing before him, he marveled at her beauty. She pulled out her ponytail, and her golden hair flowed over her shoulders, swinging forward as she bent to tug off his jeans.

He stripped his shirt over his head, and as Sophie took his pants from his ankles, she knelt in front of him, licking her lips as her gaze locked on his cock. *Holy fuck,* she was sexy.

Taking him in her hand, she lowered her head, wrapping her lips around him and sucking him. The warm, wet sensation shot electricity straight to his heart, tightening his balls as she stroked him with her mouth. He wouldn't last long like this.

He tried to speak, but his voice came out as a grunt. She released him, running her tongue from base to tip before grinning up at him. "Did you want to say something?"

"Get your ass up here and ride me like a broomstick, witch."

"Ooh. I really do love it when you talk dirty." She climbed into his lap and lowered herself onto his dick, giving him the ride of his life.

He pressed his thumb to her clit as she moved, and as she screamed his name, he lost control. They climaxed together, and she leaned into him, panting, the warmth of her breath raising goose bumps on his skin. God, he wanted this woman to be his.

"Do witches really ride broomsticks?" She sat up, resting her hands on his shoulders.

"Not that I'm aware of."

She nodded. "Good. You've ruined me for all other broomsticks, I'm afraid. Even Big Blue isn't going to cut it anymore."

"Big Blue?"

She slid off his lap and retrieved their discarded clothes, tossing him his pants. "My vibrator. The one I threatened you with a while back?"

"Ah." He chuckled and stood, stepping into his underwear. "Well, I hope to ensure you never need a toy like that again, unless we're playing with it together."

"I can't imagine wanting it...unless you and Beast are out of town." She ran her finger over his dick and wiggled her eyebrows.

"You settled on a name." He pulled on his jeans and fastened the button.

"I did. What do you think?"

"I think..." His gaze locked on a patch of tan fur growing on her shoulder.

"What?" She looked down and gasped as she covered the fur with her hand. "How long has that been there?"

"I just noticed it when you stood up. It's completely normal for a witch who's been bitten to have random patches of fur before her first full moon."

"But this'll stop once I drink the potion Jane's bringing, right? The spell will cure it?"

He tried to ignore the disappointment churning in his gut. "Yeah, I believe it will."

"I'm going to shave this before we leave."

"Wait." As he gripped her hand, his phone buzzed in his back pocket, and while he was tempted to ignore it, too much was at stake to miss a possibly important call. "Hold that thought."

He dug his phone from his pocket, and as his Alpha's number lit up the screen, he groaned inwardly. His infrequent texts of *working on it* and *might have found a lead* apparently weren't good enough for her. He'd hoped to have Jackson back to normal before reporting in, to save his friend the humiliation. "Hey, Teresa."

"We need to prepare for war."

"What? No, I found Jax." He slipped on his shoes and paced the living room. "That lead I told you about panned out. He's safe, and he doesn't hold it against the coven."

Teresa paused, and Sophie shuffled toward him, placing her hand on his arm. "You should have notified me immediately," Teresa said.

"Yes, ma'am. It's a complicated situation, but if you'll meet us at ten tonight, we can explain everything. Jackson can tell you himself."

A low growl emanated from the receiver, and Trace stiffened. His Alpha wasn't happy, which meant no one would be happy for the foreseeable future.

"This complicates matters even more. One of our pack pups, Caitlyn, was playing in her wolf form with a coven member's daughter. The witch fell into the swamp, and Caitlyn pulled her out with her teeth. She saved the little girl's life, but she broke skin."

"Shit."

"The witchling is already showing signs of the mutation, and the full moon is tonight. They're claiming we arranged it in retaliation for Jackson and the curse. The high priestess is out of town, but the moment she returns, war is imminent. The pack is on edge, ready to strike first."

"Don't let them. Meet us at the gathering point at ten. Come alone, though. This isn't something the entire pack needs to see."

CHAPTER THIRTEEN

S ophie stood in the forest, clutching Trace's hand as they waited for his Alpha to arrive. Jax sat in a pile of leaves in the center of the clearing, licking his paw and wiping it on his ear in a most cat-like way. Trace shook his head, grumbling under his breath, and Sophie rubbed his arm.

"He'll be okay. We'll fix this." She tried to reassure him with her eyes, but he must've sensed her unease. Yes, she was a fauna witch, and if she had even a quarter of her grandma's power, with proper training she could have fixed Jax hog-tied with her eyes closed. But therein lay the problem. Sophie wasn't trained.

They were relying on a self-proclaimed bad witch, someone who had botched more spells than she could count, to focus Sophie's magic and send it into Jax. And now Trace's Alpha was on her way.

With a deep inhale, he straightened his spine and nodded. "You're right. If anyone can fix this, it's you. You're going to be a phenomenal witch."

If she stayed a witch. Jane had texted at sundown that

they were on their way, but Austin was five hundred miles away. Even if Gaston drove like he was racing a Grand Prix, they still might not make it before midnight.

"Maybe we should do the spell now, before Teresa gets here." Sophie squeezed his hand and released it. "I'm nervous enough without an audience."

"Don't be." Crimson took the potion bottle from her pocket and shook it. "I can channel magic all day long. It's only my own spells that I screw up."

*Not the slightest bit reassuring.* A nervous giggle bubbled from Sophie's throat. "Wasn't the whole point of this to keep the pack and the coven from finding out what happened?"

"Teresa needs to see this with her own eyes, to understand it was an accident, so she can calm the pack down. If they attack before the leaders sit down to discuss it, we're doomed."

"'Doomed.'" Sophie shuddered. "Now there's a dramatic word. Can't you say 'screwed' or 'fucked'? It would sound less ominous."

A woman with dark brown hair and hazel eyes approached from the swamp. "I'm afraid everything about this situation is ominous." She wore Army-green cargo pants and a tight black t-shirt with combat boots.

A whimper escaped from Sophie's throat, and she could only assume it was the developing wolf inside her reacting to the Alpha's presence. The sadness in Trace's eyes as he held her hand confirmed it.

"Teresa, this is Sophie and Crimson." Trace gestured to each of them. "And that's Jackson." He pointed to the cat.

Teresa's eyes widened as she knelt in front of him. "Jax, is that really you?"

The cat meowed in response, and Teresa shot to her

feet before stomping toward Sophie. "So the witch you tried to defend was the culprit after all."

Sophie had the sudden urge to lie on her back and show her belly to the woman, as if that would help the situation, but she squared her shoulders and faced the Alpha. "I didn't do it." The moment the woman's eyes met hers, Sophie was tempted to cower. Instead, she moved next to Trace, seeking comfort in his support.

He wrapped an arm around her shoulders, holding her close to his side. "Apart from being in the wrong place at the wrong time, Sophie had nothing to do with it."

"In bed with the enemy again? Are we having a repeat of the nymph incident?" Teresa narrowed her eyes. "What spell did you put on him?"

Again? The nymph incident? "So that's why you didn't want to elaborate on that story."

Trace huffed. "This isn't about me."

"I did it." Crimson stepped forward. "I accidentally turned Jax into a cat." She explained the sex game and the resulting so-called curse she inadvertently put on the pack. "I had no idea it was affecting all of you."

Teresa glared at Trace. "Why was this not reported the moment you found out?"

"Look at the guy. He's humiliated." Trace paused, expecting her to admonish him for his tone. When she didn't, he continued, "How do you think the rest of the pack will treat him if they find out he voluntarily let a witch turn him into a cat? He'll lose their respect, lose his rank."

She crossed her arms. "I see your point. How are you going to remedy it?"

"The witches have a spell. Let them work their magic, and then you can take Jackson back to the pack. Tell them he had amnesia. Let them see him alive and well, and they'll have nothing to go to war over."

"Nothing but the fact that one of ours bit one of theirs."

"The truce has been in place for a hundred years. I'm sure you can work it out with the coven. If the parents are calm, the high priestess won't go to war over it."

"Maybe, but tempers are already running high." Teresa bowed her head at Sophie. "My apologies for accusing you. If you can return him to his natural form, the pack will be in your debt."

Crimson tossed Sophie the potion bottle and rubbed her hands together. "Let's do this."

Sophie sprinkled the potion on Jax, who answered with an offended hiss. "Do you want to be a cat forever?" Sophie scolded. "Chill."

Crimson handed Sophie her grandmother's hand-written incantation, and Sophie tried not to picture the corpse she'd used to write it. It was an image she couldn't unsee. With Crimson's hands sandwiching her head, Sophie scanned the words on the page, then read them aloud.

*"A simple mistake made difficult to break.*
*With this potion, I set in motion*
*a spell to reverse your current hell."*

Something in her core popped and fizzed, like a can of soda that had been shaken before it was opened. The fizziness had to be the magic, but it flowed up to her shoulders and down to her hips, threatening to spread out to her limbs. She tried to gather it up, to focus it into Jax, but the magic foam slipped through her metaphorical fingers, and panic began to flush it out.

"Hold on, honey. I got it." Crimson did something. Whatever it was, it pulled the fizzy magic back into a ball inside Sophie's chest. Crimson lifted Sophie's arm, and the foam rolled down, past her elbow and out her fingertips, slapping Jax and knocking him over as if he'd been struck by a car.

Crimson released her, and Sophie gasped, slumping into Trace's side as nausea threatened to give her dinner a reappearance. "Nobody told me spell-casting hurts." She rubbed her burning chest, letting Trace carry most of her weight.

"The big ones always do," Crimson said. "You get used to it."

Get used to pain? No thanks.

Jackson lifted his kitty head, blinking his feline eyes, and Sophie's heart sank. "It didn't work."

"Give it a minute," Crimson said.

A fog gathered around Jackson's form, and golden flecks danced in a swirling pattern above him before swooping down like a tornado and enveloping him in sparkling magic. As the storm dissipated, a man stood in the leaf pile. He had dark brown hair and brown eyes...the same man from the unfinished painting in Crimson's loft.

He was muscular like Trace, though not as big and not quite as hairy. Sophie's gaze traveled down over chiseled abs, and *oh my word.* "Well, that answers my question. All werewolves are hung like horses. Damn. Did anyone think to bring him some clothes?"

Trace took off his jacket and offered it to Jackson. "It's good to have you back, buddy."

Jax refused the clothing. "It's good to be back. Teresa." He glanced at the Alpha before lowering his gaze. "Everything they told you was true. My own embarrassment stopped me from seeking help from the pack, and I realize now that was a mistake. I will accept whatever punishment you deem fit for my crimes."

Teresa nodded. "Right now, you need to head home, get some clothes, and meet me at the den. We've got a pack to settle down."

"Yes, ma'am. Thanks for your help, guys. Crimson... I'll uh. I'll call you." He shifted into his wolf form and bounded away.

Crimson shook her head. "That boy's never going to call me again."

Sophie laughed. "Can you blame him?"

"Not really."

"Sophie!" Jane appeared in the clearing and ran toward her, but she only made it three steps before her heels sank into the soft earth and her ankle twisted. She stumbled, stepping out of her shoes and continuing the trek barefoot. "You could have told me we were meeting you in the middle of the swamp. I'd have dressed for the occasion."

"I thought you knew werewolves were the outdoorsy type." Sophie forced a smile, her apprehension stopping it from being genuine.

"You know them better than I do. Now, who's your favorite vampire in the whole wide world?" Jane held up a corked glass bottle. "I had to ask my father for help obtaining this, and you *know* how I feel about asking him for help."

Trace gave Sophie's shoulder a squeeze before he released her and paced to the edge of the clearing with his Alpha. They talked in hushed voices, and if she tried,

Sophie might have been able to make out what they said. She didn't need to hear their words to understand Trace's disappointment.

Jane had come through with time to spare, which, deep down, Sophie knew she would. If she drank it now, it would stop the werewolf mutation, and she'd remain a witch for the rest of her life. She glanced at Trace, catching his gaze, but he didn't smile.

Sophie took the potion from Jane. "Thanks, babe. I owe you one."

"If you knew what I went through to get that, you'd think it's worth at least twenty, but we'll call it even. Consider it an engagement present. All your dreams are coming true."

"You're right. They are." Sophie peered at the pale blue potion in her hand, a feeling of resolve washing over her. "I finally understand the last line of my grandmother's prophecy."

"What does it mean?"

She looked at Jane. "I've found everything, and I have to lose it all. I have to lose my magic."

"What?" Jane looked at her like she was crazy, and maybe she was. But Sophie knew what she had to do.

Turning on her heel, she marched toward Trace, her long strides quickening into a jog as she neared him. Teresa grimaced at her phone, and Trace's expression was solemn.

"The witch's parents are starting to freak," he said. "It's an hour until midnight, and she's starting to grow fur."

"Here." Sophie handed the bottle to Teresa.

"What's this?"

"It's a potion that will stop the mutation. Get it to the girl and have her drink it before midnight."

Teresa stared at the potion, a look of awe in her eyes. "Where did you get this? My entire life, I've only heard of two witches capable of creating such a spell."

"One of them was my grandmother. Consider it a peace offering. If I'm going to join your pack, I want everyone to know there are no hard feelings."

"Sophie." Trace shook his head.

"Go." Sophie gripped Teresa's shoulder. "You're running out of time."

"Thank you." Teresa bowed her head and then sprinted into the trees.

Trace swallowed hard, his lips twitching as an array of emotions crossed his face. Taking her shoulders in his hands, he let his gaze roam around her face, his feelings seeming to seep into her body through his eyes and his touch. "You gave up your chance to have all your dreams come true to save a little girl and keep the peace in my pack. You never cease to amaze me."

"Becoming a witch was *a* dream, but it wasn't *all* of them. It definitely wasn't my innermost dream." She tapped a finger to his chest. "The one you're supposed to make come true."

He raised his eyebrows, silently urging her to continue.

"I thought I wanted to become a witch and have magical powers and all that jazz, but what it really boils down to is…my innermost dream has been right in front of me all along. All I've wanted all my life is to belong somewhere. To have a group of people I can count on and a place that feels like home. I already have that here with you. I don't need to be able to cast spells. Besides, magic kinda hurts."

He shook his head, still unbelieving. "You're going to turn into a werewolf."

"I know. Will your pack accept me?"

"Of course they will. You'll be one of us, and…" He pressed his lips together.

"And?"

"And you'll be with me. I love you, Sophie."

She stepped into his arms and wrapped hers around his waist as she glimpsed Jane and Crimson standing off to the side. Crimson gave her two thumbs up, and Jane clutched her hands over her chest, making heart eyes at them.

"You mentioned some perks to werewolves mating within their species." She brushed a kiss to his lips. "What are they?"

"Our strength doubles."

"Mmm… Stamina too? Not that you're lacking." She laced her fingers behind his neck.

He chuckled. "I guess we'll have to find out."

"Anything else?"

"Mated werewolves stop aging. Not completely, but it slows tremendously. Teresa is a hundred and fifty."

Sophie gaped. "She doesn't look a day over thirty!"

Jane snickered. "You should have told her that from the get-go. It would've saved you both a lot of trouble."

"Go ahead and laugh." Sophie pulled a face over her shoulder at her friend. "This just means I'll be around to taunt you forever and ever."

"I'm looking forward to every minute of it." Jane hugged them both. "You've got ten minutes before you sprout fur and howl at the moon with your man. Call me later and let me know how it goes." She turned to Crimson. "How about that drink we talked about?"

Crimson smiled. "I'm down. See you later, Sophie."

As her friends left the clearing, Sophie looked into Trace's dark honey eyes and grinned. "I'm going to be a werewolf."

"A wolf I'd like to *wear* all night."

She laughed. "Are you *aware* of the pun you just made, wolf?"

His face turned serious. "Are you aware that I want to spend the rest of my life with you, which will be a really, *really* long time if you agree."

"I am."

"Will you be my mate?"

"I will."

He grinned wickedly. "Good, now take off your clothes so we can howl at the moon."

EPILOGUE

Turning into a wolf wasn't as weird as Sophie imagined it would be. Once the fur sprouted over her entire body, it wasn't the slightest bit embarrassing. In fact, from the look in Trace's eyes, she must have been the hottest wolf in the forest.

Hunting wasn't as icky as she expected either. Trace took her through the woods, searching for prey, and once she figured out how to let go and let the wolf part of her take the lead, she caught her dinner and satiated the canine hunger like she was made to be a wolf.

After the hunt, they ran. And ran and ran. No wonder Trace was solid, sexy muscle. Sophie hadn't exercised this hard since she tried losing five pounds the week before her high school prom. Of course, then she'd overdone it, pulled a muscle and limped her way through the school dance. Tonight, she was a beast. Literally.

They ran for hours, never tiring, and only stopping for a drink from a nearby stream. As they circled back around, Trace poured on the speed, pouncing on her, and they tumbled through the grass until a small cabin came into view. It had a wrap-around porch and brown shuttered windows, and Sophie knew without even having to ask him with her thoughts, it was Trace's home.

She looked at him, and he sent his thoughts to her mind. *"If you're ready to stand upright again, we can go inside and test your stamina theory."*

Sophie gazed at the full moon, shining brightly above the cabin, and a calmness washed over her. Here, in the forest with Trace, was exactly where she belonged. Giddy happiness bubbled in her core and came out in a beautiful howl.

Trace howled along with her, until the faint sound of other wolves howling in the distance drifted on the air. Everything about this moment felt right. There was no reason to end it by going inside. Instead, she focused, and though she'd never been taught how to shift, she just did it, as if it were ingrained in her soul.

Trace's canine eyebrows shot up as he took in her form lying naked in the grass, and he shifted quickly before covering her body with his and making love to her beneath the moon.

---

Sophie was fully accepted and integrated into the pack. She split her nights between Trace's house on the outskirts of town and her apartment in the French Quarter, and her new duties in the pack, along with her dog-walking business, kept her so busy, she couldn't tell her head from her tail.

Two weeks after her first shift, she finally had a moment to breathe, so she did what any newly-turned werewolf woman would do and had a girls night out with a witch and a vampire. She met Jane at Evangeline's Coffee Shop ten minutes before closing and sat on a barstool next to her BFF while Crimson closed up.

"I had my first peace-keeping assignment yesterday." She straightened a stack of napkins on the counter.

"And how did it go?" Jane asked.

Crimson slid onto the stool next to her. "Oh, yeah. Tell us all about it."

Sophie shrugged. "It was rather uneventful. There's a group of bobcat shifter sisters who like to get into it with the wolves every now and then. Trace says the meetings usually involve lots of shouting, and sometimes they meet up after and fight."

Jane's eyes widened. "Don't tell me you had to fight a bobcat."

"Oh, goodness, no. You know me better than that. All I had to do was remind them to chill out every now and then, and they actually came to an agreement over territory. First time in thirty years, so I hear."

"Wow." Crimson smiled. "Look at you, already an asset to your pack."

"She makes a great werewolf, doesn't she?" Jane asked.

"Definitely." Crimson stood. "Are you ladies ready to go?"

As Sophie and Jane followed Crimson toward the front door, a short, heavy-set woman strutted through. She wore black leggings and a deep burgundy tunic, and her dark hair hung in long braids around her shoulders.

Crimson froze, gripping Sophie's arm until her nails dug into her skin. "Fuck me," she whispered under her breath. "That's the high priestess."

The woman stopped in front of Crimson and shoved a

white card toward her. "You're summoned to be judged by the council of elders."

Crimson took the card. "Judged for what?"

"Misuse of magic, lying under oath, conspiracy with the werewolves…" She ticked the items off on her fingers. "You're lucky I'm listening to my advisors, or I'd have bound your magic already."

"What misuse of magic?" Jane crossed her arms. "She hasn't done anything wrong."

"Tell that to the werewolf she turned into a cat."

Sophie's mouth dropped open. "How did you know that? The pack swore to secrecy."

The priestess raked her gaze over Sophie and lifted one shoulder in a dismissive shrug. "Her ex-lover has a thirteen-year-old sister. Teens love to talk. Word got back to the coven." She turned to Crimson. "Lying under oath is reason enough to bind your powers on its own."

"I didn't lie." Crimson straightened her spine. "You specifically asked if I'd kidnapped or killed a werewolf or put a curse on their pack. Jackson stayed with me willingly after the accident, and I had no idea my attempts to undo the spell were affecting the others."

"That's true." Sophie nodded. "She didn't know."

"You will appear before the council for judgment tomorrow. If you fail to show, we will consider it an admission of guilt." She leaned closer and lowered her voice. "And I can't wait to find you guilty." She turned on her heel and marched out the door.

Sophie and Jane scanned the accusations listed on the card in Crimson's trembling hand, and Sophie rubbed her back. "It'll be okay. We'll get you through this."

Crimson pressed her lips into a thin line and shook her head. "I'm screwed."

# ABOUT THE AUTHOR

Carrie Pulkinen is a paranormal romance author who has always been fascinated with things that go bump in the night. Of course, when you grow up next door to a cemetery, the dead (and the undead) are hard to ignore. Pair that with her passion for writing and her love of a good happily-ever-after, and becoming a paranormal romance author seems like the only logical career choice.

Before she decided to turn her love of the written word into a career, Carrie spent the first part of her professional life as a high school journalism and yearbook teacher. She loves good chocolate and bad puns, and in her free time, she likes to read, drink wine, and travel with her family.

*Connect with Carrie online:*
www.CarriePulkinen.com